KING ARTHUR

THE
& LEGENDS
OF CAMELOT

KING ARTHUR

THE & LEGENDS OF CAMELOT

MOLLY PERHAM

ILLUSTRATED BY JULEK HELLER

VIKING

VIKING
Published by the Penguin Group
Penguin Books USA Inc., 375 Hudson Street, New York, New York 10014, U.S.A.
Penguin Books Ltd, 27 Wrights Lane, London W8 5TZ, England
Penguin Books Australia Ltd, Ringwood, Victoria, Australia
Penguin Books Canada Ltd, 10 Alcorn Avenue, Toronto, Ontario, Canada M4V 3B2
Penguin Books (N.Z.) Ltd, 182–190 Wairau Road, Auckland 10, New Zealand

Penguin Books Ltd, Registered Offices: Harmondsworth, Middlesex, England

This edition first published simultaneously in 1993
in the United States of America by Penguin Books USA Inc.
and in Great Britain by Dragon's World Ltd

Text copyright © Molly Perham 1993
Illustrations copyright © Julek Heller 1990 & 1993
All rights reserved

Library of Congress Catalog Card Number:
92– 61762

ISBN 0-670-84990-1

Typeset by DQP in Bembo
Printed in Hong Kong

CONTENTS

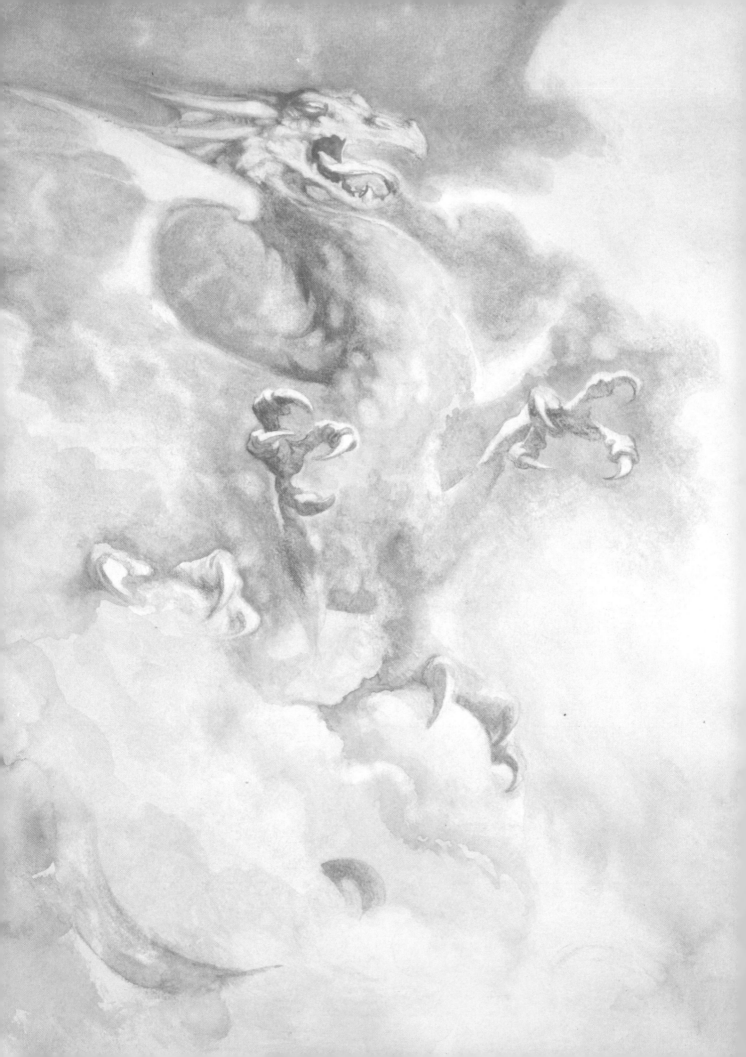

MERLIN THE MAGICIAN

MANY CENTURIES ago Britain was a place of magic and superstition. Witches, giants and dragons inhabited the thick forests that covered much of the land. Merlin was a magician whose wisdom and power were greatly respected by all the people. No one really knew who he was or where he came from, but it was rumored that he was the son of a Cornish princess and an angel who had fallen out of favor with the gods. He was brought up by the Druids, from whom he learned astrology, spell-making, and how to change shape. From his unknown father he inherited the gift of second sight.

Those were dangerous, turbulent times, when everyone lived in fear and confusion. For years the Britons had been under Roman rule, and when the legions finally left to return to their homeland, fighting broke out between all the different tribes. The people prayed that a great leader might be sent to unite them so that there would be peace in the land. But evil Vortigern killed his chief enemy, the good and noble Constantine, and made himself King. Vortigern's forces ruthlessly slew anyone who stood in their way and years of bloodshed followed.

When the Saxons invaded from across the North Sea and drove the Britons out from their homes, Vortigern fled with his army to the mountains of Wales. There he decided to build a strong tower to protect himself from the savage warriors. He ordered his men to collect together a great pile of stones and build a castle on top of Snowdon, the highest mountain of all. But though they worked hard, the masons did not make much progress. Each night, when darkness fell, all the stones that they had piled up during the day fell down again. After several weeks the workmen went to the King and told him that the job could not be done.

Vortigern was dismayed when he heard this. He sent for all the wise men and wizards that he knew and asked them how he should build his castle. They consulted together, and eventually told the King that he must find a man who had no earthly father. This man's blood should be mixed with the mortar that the masons were using, and then the walls would be strong and not fall down.

Messengers were sent out all over the country to find such a man, and eventually they found Merlin and took him to the King. Vortigern was delighted when Merlin was brought to him: he thought he had found means to make his castle strong.

But Merlin laughed when he heard what was required of him. "My blood will not hold the stones together," he said scornfully. "Who are these fools that told you so?"

Vortigern sent for the wise men again. "Tell me," said Merlin, "why do you think the King's castle keeps falling down?"

The wise men looked at each other in embarrassed silence.

Then Merlin said, "Well, if you don't know why it falls down, how do you know that my blood will make it strong?"

Still the wise men did not speak, so Merlin turned to the King and said, "There is a deep pool underneath the foundations of your castle. You will find the cause of all the trouble hidden in the water. Get your men to dig down deep, and you will see that I am right."

Vortigern was anxious to see how much this strange man knew, so he told his men to dig as Merlin directed. And sure enough, when they had gone down deep enough, they found there was a pool of water beneath the ground on which they had been trying to build the castle.

Merlin stepped forward and turned to the wise men again. "Now tell us what is hidden in the dark waters of this pool," he commanded.

But the wise men did not dare say a word. They had no idea what might be hidden in the water, and they were afraid of this bearded old man who seemed to know so much more than they did.

So Merlin said to the King, "Tell your men to dig trenches and drain the water from the pool. Then you will find two dragons at the bottom – one white and the other red. During the day these monsters sleep peacefully but at night they fight and shake the ground and make your castle fall down."

When the water had been drained off, there lay the two dragons, just as Merlin had said.

Vortigern realized that Merlin was much wiser than those men he had previously trusted and so he asked him about the future.

"The white dragon symbolizes the Saxons and the red the Britons," Merlin answered. "They will fight in mortal combat until one of them wins."

"And what will happen to me?" Vortigern demanded.

Merlin had nothing good to tell him. "You have done a great deal of evil, and now evil will come to you. Constantine's sons, Aurelius and Uther, will return from exile to avenge their father's death and take the crown from your head. Aurelius will be king for a short time, and then his brother Uther will rule. And after Uther there will come a king greater than any that has reigned in England before, or will ever reign again."

Vortigern was terrified when he heard these words and he fled with his men to another castle in the mountains. He fortified the walls as strongly as he could, hoping to protect himself from the fate that Merlin had prophesied. But the two brothers, Aurelius and Uther, marched against him with a huge army and burned the castle to the ground. Vortigern perished in the flames.

Then Aurelius turned his attention to the pagan Saxons who were pillaging the countryside, burning the churches and terrorizing the people. He fought many battles and eventually managed to overcome them.

The knights wanted to crown Aurelius immediately. But before he would allow them to make him king, Aurelius planned to build a monument to all the brave men who had been killed by the heathen tribes.

"First of all," he said, "I will rebuild all the churches and monasteries that have been destroyed by the enemy. And when that is done I will put up a memorial that will last until the end of the world."

Aurelius sent for Merlin and asked for his help. When Merlin heard that Aurelius wanted to build a monument that would last for ever he told him about some stones in Ireland that would be just right for the job.

"Once upon a time," he said, "there was a giant in Ireland who wanted to build a circle of stones. He carried the stones himself, all the way from Africa. They are so huge that an ordinary man cannot move even one of them."

"Then how will we bring them over to this country, if they are so heavy?" asked Aurelius. "In any case, why do we need to get stones from Ireland, when we have plenty here already?"

"Yes, but we don't have stones like these," Merlin explained. "They are magic stones. If anyone who is sick bathes in water with which the stones have been washed, they will become well again. There are no stones anywhere else in the world that would make such an excellent monument to those men who died fighting for the freedom of our country."

The knights were eager to send for these wonderful stones, so ships were prepared and Uther, the King's brother, was made captain of the fleet. Merlin went with them to bring back the magic stones from across the sea.

When the ships reached Ireland and the Irish people heard why the Britons had come to their country they pelted them with stones. Those stones, they said, were the only ones the intruders could carry away. But when Uther and the knights advanced on them they fled, and Merlin led the way to the mountain of Kildare, on top of which the stones lay.

The Britons had never seen such large stones before and they stared at them doubtfully, wondering how they would carry them across the sea. But Merlin cast a spell on the huge blocks, so that despite their size they became as light as pebbles. Then the knights were able to lift them easily and carry them to the waiting ships.

The fleet set sail for England again, and when they landed the stones were taken to a place where many men had been massacred by the heathen invaders. Once they had been put into position Merlin's magic wore off and they became heavy again, so that no man could move even the smallest one from the place where it had been put.

Aurelius came from London to dedicate the stones to the memory of the men who had fallen. Then a great feast was prepared and Aurelius was crowned King.

All this was such a long time ago that people have forgotten now exactly how it happened. But in the south of England, on Salisbury Plain near Winchester, there is to this day a circle of enormous stones that is called Stonehenge. Some people say that these are the magic stones that Merlin brought over from Ireland, so that Aurelius could build a monument that would last until the end of the world.

KING UTHER AND IGRAINE

A S MERLIN had prophesied, Aurelius did not reign for long. Soon after he had been crowned, he fell ill and died. His brother Uther was then proclaimed King Uther of Britain. Uther's kingdom stretched from London and Winchester – which was then called Camelot – to Cornwall, at the farthest tip of the land. Merlin the magician, who had been made the King's chief adviser, rode with him as he travelled about the realm. One summer evening, as the two men rode along the edge of a cliff above the sea, they saw on the horizon a billowing cloud in the shape of a dragon.

Uther was mesmerized by its fiery redness against the fading light. Such a spectacular sight could only be a sign from heaven. "What does it mean?" he asked.

"It means that your son will grow up to be even greater than you are," Merlin replied. "He will be the greatest king that ever reigned."

From that moment on Uther called himself Pendragon, meaning "dragon's head," out of respect for his unborn son.

Uther wanted unity and peace in his kingdom, so he invited all the knights who had been troublesome in the past to come to court. He prepared a great feast and arranged jousting tournaments to entertain them. Among the guests were Gorlois the Duke of Cornwall, and his beautiful wife Igraine. They brought with them their two eldest daughters, Margawse and Elaine, hoping that one of them would be chosen as a bride for the King.

But Uther fell deeply in love with the lovely Igraine. Although she had grown-up daughters, Igraine's beauty was still as fresh as the morning dew and she was as slender as a young girl. Uther danced all night with her clasped in his arms and in the morning sent lavish gifts of jewels to her room.

Gorlois was jealous of the attention the King was paying to Igraine. He gathered his entourage together and took his wife and daughters back home to Tintagel Castle. At once Uther issued an ultimatum: if the Duke did not return to court with his wife within fourteen days, then the King would declare war.

Gorlois was furious when he received this message. He called his three daughters into the great hall of the castle.

"I have no son to protect my good name and follow after me, so I am asking you, my daughters, to promise that if I should die in battle against the King you will avenge my death."

Margawse and Elaine swore that they would do as he asked. And Morgan le Fay, his youngest and favorite daughter, swore that if her beloved father was killed by Uther's army, then she would take revenge on everyone of Uther's blood.

Igraine sat alone in her chamber, huddled in furs to keep herself warm. She was a good and gentle woman, who would never deceive her husband, not even for the King. As she gazed into the flickering flames of the fire that burned in the hearth she remembered the prophecy of an old woman who had once taken shelter at her father's castle. The woman said that the child Igraine would grow up to be a great beauty, and that all men who fell in love with her would come to an untimely end. Now it looked as though that prophecy might come true.

Gorlois left his wife and daughters at Tintagel. The castle's clifftop position meant it could be defended by only a handful of men. He himself made his way to Terrabil Castle, where he prepared strong fortifications against the King's attack. It was the depths of winter, and so cold that even the birds had stopped singing. Uther set up his pavilions on the bleak, exposed plain that surrounded the castle and prepared to lay siege until Gorlois was forced to surrender. Every day the Duke's warriors marched out from Terrabil to fight against the King's forces. But the two sides were evenly matched in number and fighting skills. So, although there were some fierce skirmishes and several soldiers were killed, little progress was made on either side.

Uther's love for Igraine grew stronger and stronger, and he yearned so desperately to see her that he started to fall ill. The knights, anxious for their King's health, decided that Merlin was the only person who could help him. Two of them set off on horseback to look for Merlin in the forest.

They searched for several days until one evening they met an old beggar man. "Who are you looking for?" the beggar asked.

"We are looking for Merlin, who lives in this forest around here," they replied. "The King is sick with love for the Lady Igraine and we don't know how to make him well again."

"Go back to the King and tell him that Merlin is on his way," the beggar commanded.

The knights rode as fast as they could but by the time they arrived at the King's camp with the message, Merlin was already there.

Merlin knew Uther would never be well again until Igraine was his. But he must pay a high price for taking another man's wife.

"I know what is in your heart," he said, "and if you swear on your honor to do as I ask, then Igraine will be yours."

"I will do anything," Uther sighed in despair. "Anything that is asked of me. I will even forfeit my kingdom if only I can be with my love."

"You will go to Igraine tonight," Merlin told him. "A son will be conceived, but you must promise that, as soon as he is born, you will give him to me so that I can take him to a place where he will be brought up in safety. Do you swear to this?"

"Whatever you say," Uther nodded in agreement.

Then Merlin wove a magic mist around Uther so that he took on the appearance of Gorlois. He changed himself to look like one of the Duke's men. As soon as darkness fell the two men mounted their horses and galloped towards Tintagel. The guards at the castle gates thought that Uther was the Duke of Cornwall, so they let

him through. Igraine also mistook the King for her husband and went with him to her chamber. Only the dog knew that this was not his master, but Merlin quietened his barking with a sorcerer's spell.

That night the Duke of Cornwall was killed in a raid against the King's camp. When Igraine heard the news she was distraught. If Gorlois was dead, who was the stranger she had taken to her chamber?

Peace was made between the two armies, and after a period of mourning had passed, Uther proposed marriage. Igraine told him that she was expecting a child, and therefore could not be his wife.

Uther asked her whose child it was, and at first she was too ashamed to answer.

"Don't be afraid," said the King. "Tell me the truth and I will love you even more."

So Igraine told him what had happened on the night that her husband was killed, and confessed that she did not know who was the father of her child.

Uther then explained that he had been her mysterious visitor, and that the child she was expecting was his. He told how Merlin had prophesied that his son would be the greatest King who ever reigned.

When she heard this Igraine agreed to become Uther's wife. As the months passed she grew large with child and in due time gave birth to a son.

Igraine wept as she gazed down at the tiny baby in her arms. She could not bear the thought of parting from her only son. But Uther had promised Merlin that as soon as the baby was born he would be given into the magician's care. Uther wrapped the infant in a cloth of gold and handed him over to Merlin, who had come to the castle gate in his disguise as a poor beggar man.

Morgan le Fay, Igraine's youngest daughter, was the only person who saw this happen. She had been with her mother at the time of the birth and saw how much it pained Igraine to part with the new-born child. She alone knew that the King was lying when he announced to the court that the prince had been born dead.

Merlin took the baby to the home of Sir Ector, a good and honest knight who lived some distance from Tintagel Castle. He knew that Ector and his wife would look after the boy well and treat him as though he was their own son. Ector's wife had recently weaned her own son, Kay, and she immediately put the baby to suckle at her breast.

Before Merlin left Sir Ector's castle he summoned a priest and had the child christened. He called him Arthur.

Uther Pendragon had only a few years' happiness with the beautiful Igraine. The Saxons started attacking again, and sent a traitor to Tintagel Castle who poisoned the King and many of his followers. Uther was so desperately ill that he was unable to speak and name an heir. When he died the knights started quarrelling among themselves about who should rule. None of them knew that many miles away Uther's son was growing up into a fine young man.

Soon the knights were fighting among themselves, and the kingdom fell into chaos once more. The Saxons, seeing that there was no man strong enough to lead the Britons against them, conquered more and more of the land.

After several years of bloodshed and misery Merlin decided that Arthur was old enough to take his place on the throne. He advised the Archbishop of Canterbury to invite all the lords and knights to a gathering in London on Christmas Day.

"A miracle," Merlin declared, "will reveal the rightful King."

THE SWORD
IN THE STONE

ARTHUR WAS brought up in the safety of Sir Ector's household and treated as if he was one of the family. The two boys took lessons in the skills needed to become a knight. They were taught chivalry and Latin and the terminology of the chase. They learned how to shoot a straight arrow and to wield a sword, and practised using a lance by tilting at the quintain.

When lessons were over the boys were free to gallop their horses through the fields and forests that surrounded the estate. Arthur was a fine horseman by the time he was eight. He could run like the wind and swim like a fish in the castle moat.

Merlin watched over Arthur and made sure that he came to no harm. In summer he perched in the trees disguised as a bird, or took the shape of a butterfly fluttering around the sunlit meadows. In the winter months he became a fir tree, standing guard as Arthur played in the snow and skated precariously on ice.

Kay and Arthur were like real brothers to each other. Arthur was a good-natured boy and didn't mind putting up with a little bullying. Kay, after all, was two years older than he, and was Sir Ector's natural son. Kay would soon be a squire, and then a knight. Sometimes Arthur wondered who his real parents were, and whether he too was worthy enough to be a knight. But most of the time he was too busy enjoying himself to give these matters much thought.

Hawking was the boys' favorite sport. They were allowed to take the birds out only under supervision, but Arthur spent many happy hours in the mews where they were kept, talking to them as they sat on their perches. There were a pair of little merlins, an old peregrine who was not much use in wooded country, a kestrel with which the boys had learned the rudiments of falconry, and Sir Ector's splendid hawk, called Cully. Sometimes Arthur helped the austringer, Will Hobson, to clean and repair the leather hoods and jesses. All the hoods were made in Sir Ector's colors: white leather with red baize at the sides and a tuft of blue-grey heron feathers on top.

One day Arthur was alone in the mews when Kay came in, put on one of the gauntlets, and called Cully to come down. Cully glared at him with malevolent eyes and refused to budge. Annoyed, Kay took the hawk down from his perch and covered his head with a leather hood.

"What are you doing?" Arthur asked fearfully. "You know Will doesn't allow us to handle the birds on our own."

"Hobson's only a servant," said Kay grandly. "He can't tell me what to do." He put Cully on to his arm and strode out into the courtyard.

Arthur followed him, carrying the lure. Kay was Sir Ector's son after all; he must know what he was doing.

The two boys went through the gates and over the wooden drawbridge that crossed the moat. When they reached the meadows that lay below the castle Kay took off the hood and began to undo the leash and swivel from the jesses. Cully, feeling the trappings being taken off him, raised his crest and moved his weight from one foot to the other.

"Off you go," cried Kay, throwing his arm upward. The hawk soared into the clear blue sky, revelling in his freedom. The boys watched as he circled round high above their heads until, spotting a rabbit on the ground, he swooped down to snatch up his prey. Then he landed on the branch of a tree and settled down to enjoy his meal.

But then, having eaten his fill, Cully refused to come down. He folded his wings and sat motionless, eyes closed against the midday sun.

Arthur swung the lure and Kay whistled, but still the hawk refused to move. Soon Kay lost patience.

"Let's leave him then," he said angrily, "he'll come home on his own."

"We can't do that," cried Arthur. "What would Hobson say?"

"What does it matter what Hobson says?" said Kay in a sulky voice. "It's not his hawk; it's Father's."

"But he trained Cully. It would break Will's heart if we lost his pet. Anyway, he's responsible for the birds."

"That's his problem." Kay started to walk off in the direction of the castle. "You can get the stupid bird down yourself if you are so fond of it."

Arthur stared miserably at Kay's retreating back. They would certainly be punished for losing Sir Ector's favorite hawk. What was he to do? He had better sit still and leave the lure on the ground so that Cully could come down in his own good time. But Cully showed no intention of doing this. He had eaten a good meal and was not feeling hungry. Arthur resigned himself to missing his own lunch: he was in for a long wait.

After what seemed like hours the hawk stirred and opened one eye. He ruffled his feathers and suddenly took off into the forest. Arthur leapt to his feet and ran after him, deeper and deeper into the undergrowth until the sun no longer shone with dappled light through the trees.

Arthur had never been alone in the forest before, and to make matters worse it would soon be night. He thought about all the wild beasts that came out in the dark, and the bands of Saxon outlaws who attacked innocent passers-by. He remembered stories about magicians that cast evil spells and dragons that lived under rocks. He wished that he was back at the castle, but was determined not to give in until he had captured the hawk. Hobson had once told him that if a bird spent a whole night in freedom it would become wild again. He couldn't allow that to happen.

At last Cully perched in a tree to roost. Perhaps, thought Arthur hopefully, I could remember this spot and go back to the castle to fetch Will.

He began to fight
his way back through
the bushes, but it was
not long before he was too
tired to go any further. He sat
down on a pile of leaves to rest and
promptly fell asleep.

All night long Merlin watched over
the sleeping boy. If a wild animal threatened to
attack he turned it into stone. Arthur slept
peacefully and it was several hours after dawn when
he finally woke up and stretched. At first he could not
remember where he was. Then as soon as he recalled
what had happened the day before, he wished he had
remained asleep. He looked around anxiously, hoping to see
Cully perched somewhere nearby. But there was no sign of the
hawk and Arthur did not recognize anything around him. Even
the plants and animals seemed unfamiliar.

The boy sat very still and listened to the sounds of the forest.
Strangely, he no longer felt afraid. The branches of the trees swished gently
to and fro in the breeze and the air seemed to be full of bird song. He could
hear the sound of a stream trickling nearby, and decided to set off in that
direction. At least he would have some water to drink.

Arthur came out into a clearing in the forest and the first thing he
saw was a tumbledown cottage. Somebody obviously lived there, because
smoke curled out from a hole in the thatched roof. Bending over the stream
that ran close by was an old beggar man with white hair and a long straggly
beard. He was scooping up water in an iron bucket, and looked up as Arthur
approached.

"Excuse me, sir," said Arthur politely, "can you tell me the way to Sir
Ector's castle?"

The old man put down his bucket and looked hard at
Arthur. "Are you lost, boy?" he said.

"Well, yes, I am rather," Arthur replied.

"Would you like a drink?"

Arthur looked doubtfully at the grimy old bucket that
was being offered to him, but not wishing to hurt the old
man's feelings, he raised it to his lips and
drank.

To his surprise the water tasted like nectar, and then he realized that he was holding a golden goblet in his hands.

"And now, Arthur, I expect you would like something to eat?"

Arthur stared in surprise. "How do you know my name?" he asked.

The old man smiled and picked up a stone from the river-bed. Holding it up in the air he made a swirling movement with his other hand and the stone turned into a loaf of newly-baked bread. Another stone turned into a piece of cheese, and a third one became a ripe peach.

"Eat up, Arthur," he said, "and then we will go into my house and I will show you your future. My name is Merlin, by the way."

Arthur ate hungrily. He had eaten nothing for twenty-four hours. Perhaps hunger was causing him to have strange dreams? When he had finished eating he followed Merlin into the cottage.

This was the most marvellous place that Arthur had ever seen. It seemed much larger than it looked from outside and, unlike the sparsely-furnished chambers that he was used to in the castle, was stuffed from floor to ceiling with all kinds of interesting and extraordinary things.

There were thousands of old books bound in brown leather, some chained to shelves and others stacked in precarious piles – but all of them covered in dust, as though they had not been opened for a very long time. In every corner there were untidy heaps of ancient manuscripts, yellowing at the corners and fragile with age. There were rows of bottles in all shapes and sizes, containing strange, rainbow-colored liquids.

There were stuffed birds on the mantelpiece: popinjays and kingfishers; and a peacock with all its feathers. There were boars' tusks and rabbits' feet and the claws of tigers; six live snakes in an aquarium; two baby hedgehogs; a sheep's head and – Arthur's eyes nearly popped out of his head – a human skull.

Looking upwards through thick cobwebs Arthur saw that several bats clung to the rafters, and just then an owl flopped down from a dark corner and settled on Merlin's white head.

"Go away, Caesar," he said distractedly, "we've got important things to do." He shooed a black cat off one of the chairs and motioned Arthur to sit down.

Unrolling a scroll of parchment, Merlin examined it minutely, screwing up his eyes to read the tiny script by the light of a single candle suspended from the ceiling. He turned over several pages of a huge book that lay open on the table. The pages were filled with strange symbols and diagrams, but no words, as far as Arthur could see. Then the old man started to mutter under his breath and suddenly the room began to fill with smoke.

Arthur was alarmed at first, thinking that the house had caught fire, but then he saw that the smoke came from Merlin's mouth. Then, as he watched, it gradually began to take on a shape. It was the outline of a castle – a huge castle, much bigger than Sir Ector's or any of the other castles that Arthur had visited. It had thick stone walls and many strong towers: only a king would live in such an impenetrable fortress.

As the details became more distinct Arthur could see that a band of knights on magnificent white horses rode up a steep path to the castle gates. They carried a banner, emblazoned in gold and depicting a fiery red dragon. The knight who rode in front wore a crown, and somehow his face seemed familiar....

The dragon loomed large in front of Arthur's eyes, then wavered and disintegrated and the smoke faded away.

Arthur sat up in his own bed and rubbed his eyes. He had been having the most wonderful dream. He started to tell Kay about his strange adventures but just then someone knocked loudly at the door. Everyone in the household had to get up early that morning because they were starting the hay-making.

This was Arthur's favorite time of year. Lessons were suspended so that he and Kay could join the men out in the fields. It was all hands to the wheel to get the harvest in before the autumn rains.

Arthur loved to follow the men as they moved up and down with their scythes, cutting great swathes through the waist-high grass and sending scores of rabbits scurrying for cover into the nearby woods. He loved the smell of the new-mown hay, and the heat of the sun burning through the thin shirt on his back. He and Kay were responsible for tying the hay into sheaves and stacking them into stooks. Later these would be collected up and taken back to the barn just inside the castle gates.

Tossing the hay on to the wagon was men's work. Arthur was not yet strong enough to lift a sheaf, but Kay had grown several inches in the last few months and was almost a man. In a few weeks' time he would leave the schoolroom for good to take up his duties as a squire. Kay could toss the heavy sheaves as well as any of the farmhands. At the end of the day he would climb up on top, pulling Arthur after him, and together they would ride back to the hay barn for supper – a splendid feast of rabbit stew and apple pies which the women had been preparing for most of the day, washed down with jugs of frothing cider.

And so several more harvests came and went, and life went on much the same as usual, though it was a little dull for Arthur without his childhood companion. Kay was often away from the castle, acting as a squire to various knights at tournaments all over the country. A squire's task was to dress and arm his knight before an event, to carry all the lances, and generally to make sure that everything was kept in good order. Kay had been well trained in Sir Ector's household, and performed these tasks conscientiously. Rumor had it that Sir Ector was considering the possibility of making Kay a knight.

Meanwhile Arthur grew tall and strong and waited impatiently for his school-days to be over. This happened sooner than he expected. One day an envoy from the Archbishop arrived breathless at the castle gate with news from London.

On Christmas Day all the great nobles and knights had assembled in St. Paul's Cathedral to pray for a sign that would show who was the rightful King of England. When the service was over and they came out of the church they saw an amazing sight. There was a huge stone in the middle of the churchyard with an anvil embedded in it. Pushed into the anvil was a magnificent sword, and written in golden letters were the words:

WHOEVER PULLS THIS SWORD OUT OF THIS STONE
IS BORN TO BE KING OF ALL ENGLAND.

The nobles stood around the stone wondering about the words that were written on the sword. One of them went back to tell the Archbishop, who hurried out to see the miracle.

"God has given us a sign," he said. "We must pray once more and then those who think they are fit to be king may try to pull the sword out of the stone."

One by one the nobles tried to pull out the sword, but none of them succeeded.

"The man who will be King of England is not here," said the Archbishop. "But God will send him in his own good time."

Ten nobles were chosen to guard the sword until the right man was found. Then the Archbishop sent out messengers to all the knights in the land to invite them to a tournament.

Kay had just been made a knight, and Sir Ector agreed that this was a good opportunity for him to show off his skills. Arthur was to ride with them so he could act as Sir Kay's squire.

A very excited and expectant party set off for London that cold winter's morning. The city was crowded with visitors and they had to take lodgings some distance from the center.

On New Year's Day Sir Ector, Sir Kay and Arthur rode into town. But before they reached the field where the tournament was to be held, Kay discovered that he had forgotten his sword.

"Arthur," he gasped in horror, "I have left my sword at the house where we spent the night. I cannot fight without it. If I ride back, I will be tired before the tournament starts. Please go and get it for me."

"Of course I will," said Arthur, who was always willing to help other people. In any case, it was his duty as a squire to serve his brother.

He rode back along the road as quickly as he could, but when he reached the lodging house he found that it was locked and shuttered. The landlady and all the other people who lived there had gone to watch the jousting.

Arthur was very upset. He rode slowly back to the jousting field wondering what he could do. Without a sword Kay would not be able to take part in the tournament.

Passing St. Paul's churchyard Arthur saw a magnificent sword gleaming in the sunlight. As he drew closer he saw that it was sticking out of an anvil on top of a huge stone. Arthur looked around but saw no one. The ten knights who were supposed to be keeping watch had also gone to the tournament.

"Well," thought Arthur, "whoever owns this sword can't want it very much if they leave it lying around like that."

He dismounted from his horse and climbed onto the stone. Grasping the sword by the hilt he pulled it out of the anvil. Then, delighted to have found a sword for this brother, Arthur spurred on his horse to catch up with Sir Ector's party.

"Kay! Kay!" he called. "The lodging house was all locked up, so I couldn't fetch your sword. But I found this one pushed into an anvil. It doesn't seem to belong to anyone. Will it be all right?"

When Kay saw the sword he realized immediately what it was and the temptation was too much for him. He took it to Sir Ector.

"Father," he said, "I have the sword from the stone. Therefore I must be King of England."

Sir Ector looked at the sword and looked at Kay. He knew that his son had no right to be king. He turned and took the two boys back to the churchyard.

Putting a Bible into Kay's hand he said, "Now, my son, tell me how you got the sword."

Kay sighed. "Arthur brought it to me," he said.

"And how did you get the sword, Arthur?"

"Kay forgot his sword, and I rode back to the lodging house to get it for him," Arthur explained, hoping that he was not going to get into trouble. "But the house was all locked up. On the way back I saw this sword in the churchyard. It didn't seem to belong to anyone, so I thought that Kay might as well have it. I'm sorry if I did wrong."

"Did anyone see you take the sword?"

"No, sir, there was no one there."

"Put the sword back and let us all try to pull it out."

"But it's easy," said Arthur, "anyone could do it."

"Just do as I say," said Sir Ector sternly.

Arthur was puzzled by all this fuss over a sword, but he did as he was told and pushed it back into the anvil.

Kay seized it by the hilt, but though he pulled as hard as he could with both hands, he couldn't move it.

Then Sir Ector tried, but with no more success. "You try it, Arthur," he said.

So Arthur, wondering what this was all about, got hold of the sword and pulled it out easily.

Sir Ector stared in amazement at the boy he had brought up as his own. Then he dropped to his knees and motioned to Kay to do the same.

"Father!" Arthur cried in alarm. "Why are you kneeling before me?"

"It is God's will that whoever pulls the sword from the stone must be King of England," said Sir Ector. "You know that I am not your real father, and Kay is not your brother, although we both love you dearly. Merlin brought you to me when you were a tiny baby, wrapped in a cloth of gold. I knew you were of noble blood, but I had no idea that you were born to be King."

"If I am really King," said Arthur solemnly, "then I swear to serve God and my people, to put right any wrongs, and to bring peace to the land. But please do not leave me, Father, for I will need your support and advice. And Kay, I want you to be a knight of my court and governor of my lands."

Sir Ector and Kay promised to stay with Arthur as long as he needed them.

Then they went to the Archbishop and told him what had happened. Arthur put the sword back into the stone again and invited anyone who wished to try and pull it out. No one succeeded. Only Arthur could pull it free.

The great nobles and knights refused to agree that this unknown youth should be king over them.

"We will come again at Candlemas," they said, as they mounted their horses and rode away. "Perhaps by then a man will have been found who is more worthy to be our King."

So at Candlemas there was another great gathering, but though all the nobles tried their hardest to draw the sword, none of them could move it. Once again Arthur put his hand on the hilt and at his touch it came out as easily as though it had never been stuck fast in the stone. Yet still the nobles would not accept such a boy for their king.

"We will pray to God again," they said. And at Easter, they made another trial, but none of them could move the sword except Arthur. By now the ordinary people, who had heard of the miracle and watched the trials eagerly, would be held back no longer.

"It is God's will that Arthur should be King – we will have Arthur for our King," they cried. And so the great nobles and knights were obliged to give in.

Arthur went into the church and placed the sword on the high altar. The Archbishop took it up and touched Arthur on the shoulder with it to make him a knight. Then Arthur forgave the great nobles and knights for doubting him and swore an oath that he would be a just and true king for all his days.

He ordered the lords who held their land from the crown to fulfil the duties they owed him. Each one knelt before him in turn and promised to abide by the laws of the king. After this ceremony, Arthur said he would hear complaints about injustices and crimes committed in the land since the death of his father, Uther Pendragon. They told him of how lands and castles had been taken by force, and men murdered, and of how knights and ladies and the common people were robbed and assaulted.

Arthur ordered that all lands and properties should be returned to their rightful owners and that everyone should respect the rights of others. When that was done, Arthur organized his government. Sir Kay was made High Steward of all Britain and the most trustworthy knights were appointed to high office. Merlin was confirmed as chief counsellor to the King.

Then Arthur proclaimed that the Feast of Pentecost would be his coronation day. When that day came, the Archbishop crowned him King of all Britain. He ruled his kingdom from Camelot, and everyone rejoiced that Britain once more had a King.

MORGAN LE FAY

NOW THAT he was King, Arthur decided he must free the country from the Saxon invaders who had been terrorizing the Britons for so long. For the first few years of his reign, all his time was spent in war. Many of those nobles who had previously been doubtful about making a boy as young as Arthur their King now changed their minds, for he was such a brave and zealous ruler that he inspired all his men with courage and determination.

Soon there was peace in the southern parts of the kingdom, and with Merlin's guidance, Arthur ruled his country well. However the northern lords – the Kings of Orkney and Lothian, of Gywnedd and Powys, of Goree and Garloth – were still jealous of the unknown boy who was calling himself King of all Britain. These rebel lords travelled to Caerleon in Wales, where Arthur was holding a great feast for the Welsh people.

Arthur welcomed the lords and their knights, and sent them presents. But they refused the gifts and would not swear allegiance. They attacked Arthur as he came out of the church, and there were so many of them that the King and his followers were forced to barricade themselves into a tower.

The northern lords surrounded the tower and lay siege for fifteen days, until Merlin came out and addressed them from the steps.

"Why do you come in arms against your King?" he asked the angry knights.

"Why do we have to put up with that boy, that Arthur, as our King?" they shouted in reply.

"Listen all of you!" Merlin commanded. "Arthur is indeed your King. He is the son of Uther Pendragon. He is the rightful King of all this land – of Wales, and Ireland, and Scotland, and Orkney, too. And as the years go by his kingdom will grow beyond these isles, and he will rule other lands also."

There was silence when Merlin had finished speaking. The lords retreated and the King rode back to Camelot. But Merlin advised Arthur that it was not the last they would see of the northern rebels. Even now they were recruiting mercenaries in readiness for the next attack. It would be a good idea, Merlin counselled, if Arthur increased the strength of his fighting men before he engaged in battle against them.

Arthur sailed across the sea to France, where he hoped to enlist the help of King Ban and King Bors. They agreed to join him, and in return Arthur promised to fight for them if they found themselves in a similar situation.

The French kings with an army of 5,000 knights landed in England on All-Hallows Day. A grand tournament was held to celebrate their arrival. Even with the newcomers the northern rebels still outnumbered their combined forces. Arthur

discussed with Merlin what strategy they should adopt for the coming battle. The magician suggested that if the King's men attacked at night, they would have the advantage of surprise.

So it was that in the dead of night thousands of horsemen rode silently against the northern forces. They wore thick cloaks over their armor to stop it clanking, and the horses' hooves were muffled with sacks.

As Merlin had predicted, the rebels were unprepared for the attack. Arthur's knights charged into the northern camp slashing blindly with their swords. In the first light of dawn it was clear that thousands lay dead. The battle raged all through the next day until the men were exhausted. When only half of the King's army remained alive Merlin advised Arthur to retreat.

King Ban and King Bors returned to France and the two sides settled down to an uneasy truce.

News of Arthur's battles spread throughout his kingdom. Morgan le Fay had not seen her step-brother since he was given into the care of Merlin the Magician, but she had taken a keen interest in all his exploits. She had not forgotten that, while still a young child, she had promised her father, Gorlois the Duke of Cornwall, that if he should die at the hands of Uther Pendragon, she would avenge his death on all of Uther's blood.

When King Uther married Igraine, Morgan le Fay soon realized that she had lost her mother's affection to the King. Only when he was away in battle did Igraine pay the little girl any attention, taking her on her knee as she used to do when Gorlois was alive, and teaching her how to spin and weave. But as soon as Uther returned Morgan was banished to her rooms and forgotten until he went away again.

Then Arthur was born, and Morgan le Fay was jealous of her mother's passionate love for the new-born infant. She hated her little brother, and was pleased when he was given into Merlin's care. Igraine turned to her for comfort at this unhappy time, but seeing how close they were becoming to each other, Uther had sent the girl away from the court to a nunnery, where she studied ancient scripts and became acquainted with the mysteries of the magic arts.

As Morgan le Fay grew older she kept company with witches, who taught her their fiendish spells. Like Merlin she could see through the mists of time, far into the future, and back into the past, and could change herself at will into another form. But she used her powers destructively, manipulating men with her youth and beauty. When these skills failed her she used the blacker arts of treason and murder to bend people to her will.

So now Morgan le Fay summoned her sisters – Margawse, who was married to King Lot of Orkney, and Elaine, who was Queen of the Outer Isles – to meet at Tintagel Castle to plot against her half-brother, the King. The three sisters were as lovely as their mother, Igraine. But Morgan le Fay was the most dazzling of all. She was tall and slender, and held herself proudly erect like a noble goddess. A cloud of magnificent red-gold hair framed a face of unblemished beauty; her skin was as smooth and white as alabaster, but her eyes were hard and glinted vengefully.

Disguising herself as a pure young girl, Morgan le Fay arrived at Camelot dressed in a simple gown that accentuated her beauty. Arthur was enchanted by her innocence and loveliness. He was tired of battles and constant fighting and eager for the company of the fairer sex. He fell in love with the young maiden as soon as he saw her.

Morgan le Fay caught her breath when she saw Arthur – her baby brother had grown up with exactly the same features as his father. As she remembered how Uther Pendragon had killed her own father and alienated her mother, Morgan le Fay was consumed with hatred for the young King. But she sat next to him at dinner, daintily picking at her food and coyly accepting the choicest morsels from the King's own plate. His eyes gazed longingly into hers as they drank from the same cup.

That night Morgan le Fay lay with the King in his bedchamber. But before dawn, when Arthur stirred, she was gone from Camelot, back to the safety of her own castle.

As soon as she was certain that she was expecting a child, Morgan le Fay sent word to Arthur. He was distraught when he read the letter. He lay awake at night thinking about what had happened, and even when he managed to sleep, he was plagued by nightmares. Night after night he dreamed that dragons and serpents crawled all over his lands, killing the people and burning all the crops with their fiery breath. In his dreams he fought against them, but the more he killed the more they came, until they overcame him and he fell down dead.

Sometimes he dreamed that a youth approached him and asked why he was so sad. "I have every reason to be sad," said Arthur in his dream, "because I have seen such terrible things."

Then the youth said, "I know what you have seen. I know all your thoughts. But only a fool worries about things he can do nothing about. It is God's will that you be punished for your sin."

Arthur told Merlin about his dreams and showed him Morgan le Fay's letter. Merlin warned him that the dreams meant that evil forces would be released into the world because he had lain with his half-sister, and that a boy child would be born who would one day bring about Arthur's destruction.

"If that child survives," said Arthur fearfully, "then I am condemned to death. I have no choice but to counter the wrong done to me by committing an even greater wrong myself. May God forgive me."

When her time was near Morgan le Fay sent for her sisters. It was the early hours of May Day when they finally delivered her of a baby boy. It was a pale and sickly child that no one expected to live. But Morgan le Fay suckled the infant herself and cast many spells to ensure his survival and soon he began to thrive.

Meanwhile Arthur calculated the time that the child would be born and ordered that all male children born in his kingdom within a month of that date should be killed. A hundred infants were taken from their parents' arms, but Arthur could not bring himself to give the order to kill them.

Instead they were put into a ship and sent out to sea.

The ship got caught in a storm and was driven back to land. Just below the castle it was wrecked on some rocks and all the babies were thrown into the towering waves. But a man who lived in a hut beside the shore heard a wailing cry above the sound of the wind. He went out onto the beach and found a tiny baby wedged in a piece of wreckage from the ship. It was only just alive. Tucking the pathetic bundle under his cloak for warmth, the man carried the child home to his wife. She took the infant to her breast and suckled him.

After a few months had passed Morgan le Fay judged that Arthur would now believe that the threat to his future had been removed. She sent her trusted steward to rescue her son from the fate that had befallen him.

The once-sickly baby was now a lusty infant, plump and contented from his foster-mother's milk. Morgan le Fay was sure that the boy gurgled in recognition when he was placed in her arms. In the dead of night she wrapped him in a shawl and took him out on to the wild heath. Assuming the form of a witch, she called upon her evil friends as witnesses.

Stripping the boy of his clothing, the wicked enchantress held the naked form aloft. "I dedicate my son to the Old Powers," she declared. "He will be called Mordred. Fate has decreed that he lives to bring about his father's downfall. One day he will take his rightful place on Arthur's throne."

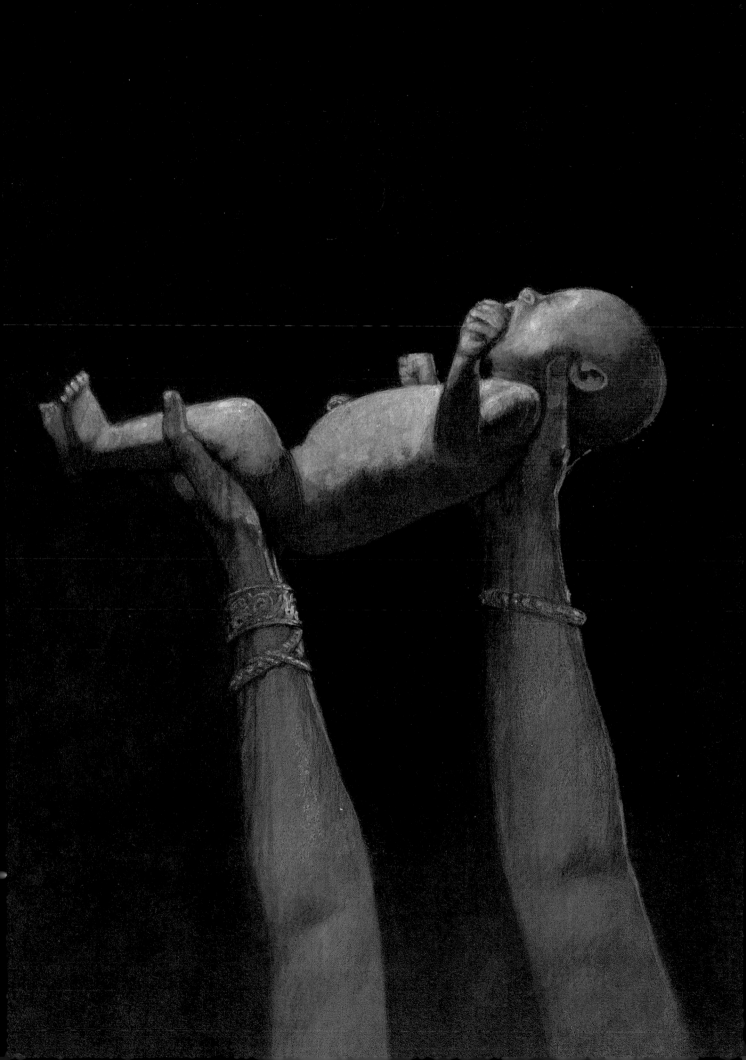

HOW ARTHUR
WON EXCALIBUR

WHEN THE French Kings Ban and Bors returned to France, the rebel lords took refuge in the city of Surhaute in King Urygens of Gorc's lands. There they rested and treated their wounds. The lords had lost many men in their battle against Arthur, so they decided to guard the borders of Wales and the north while they built up their forces once more.

Meanwhile Arthur and his knights had much to do. They labored long and hard to replace churches destroyed in the wars and to build new castles strong enough to withstand the longest siege. They guarded the coasts against invasion by marauding bands of Saxons and Picts. Every day they practised with their weapons and held regular tournaments to test their skill at arms. Soon their fame had spread throughout the land and people came from far and wide to see the armored knights on their magnificent horses.

At King Arthur's court, anyone who had been wronged or who was in danger could appeal for help. For in those far-off days, even in times of peace, there was much lawlessness. Soon everyone in the kingdom knew that Arthur and his knights could be counted on to do battle against an oppressor. Many prisoners were freed, and many ladies in distress were rescued, thanks to the bravery of King Arthur and his knights at Camelot.

But Arthur was still uneasy about the northern lords. Was it really true, if they refused to accept his claim, that he was born to be King of all England? He called Sir Ector and Merlin to him and questioned them again about his birth.

"If Uther Pendragon was my father, then who was my mother?" he asked.

They told him that his mother was Uther's wife, Igraine.

"Send for my mother so that she can tell me herself," ordered the troubled King.

Igraine was sent for and a feast was prepared in her honor in the Great Hall. All the nobles and knights and their retainers were seated at two long tables in order of their importance, while Arthur and his advisers sat at a raised table at the end, facing the assembled court.

As Igraine took her seat next to the King a knight stood up at the far end of the hall and said in a voice loud enough for everyone to hear, "I charge you, Queen Igraine, that you are the cause of all the discontent and rebellion in this kingdom. If, while Uther Pendragon was alive, you had admitted that you were Arthur's mother, there would have been no trouble. King Arthur's subjects would all have believed his claim to be King. I say that you are a false lady, and a traitor."

Everyone looked at Igraine, who sat with downcast eyes. She was silent for a while, but then she raised her head and spoke. "By Merlin's magic powers King Uther came to me in the likeness of my husband, Gorlois of Cornwall, when the Duke was already dead. That night I conceived a child. Then King Uther married me and made me his Queen. When my child was born it was taken from me and given to Merlin, wrapped in a cloth of gold. I was never told what became of my son and never even knew his name."

Sir Ector leapt to his feet. "What she says is true," he cried. He turned to look at Arthur. "Merlin brought you to me wrapped in a cloth of gold. You must be the child of Uther and Igraine."

Arthur took his mother in his arms and kissed her. He ordered that enough food and wine be brought so that the feast could continue for seven days. As they feasted and drank, musicians and singers came to entertain the King. Knights came to tell stories of their adventures and men came to seek justice for all kinds of wrongs.

One of these men was a young squire, who rode into the Great Hall leading a horse weighed down with the body of a newly-slain knight. The squire dismounted and knelt before Arthur.

"My lord, in a great forest not far from here a strange knight called King Pellinore of the Isles has set up his pavilion by a well. He challenges every passing knight who is loyal to you, and has killed my noble master. I beg you to send someone to take revenge on this warring knight."

Arthur agreed at once that justice must be done. Now at this time there was a young squire called Gryflet at King Arthur's court. His great ambition was to become a knight, and he begged to be allowed to fight with King Pellinore. Arthur was reluctant to grant this request, because Gryflet was little more than a boy, and untried in combat. But there was a rule at Camelot that the first man who asked to do a deed of great bravery must be given the quest. Arthur turned to Merlin for advice.

"Allow Gryflet his request,'"
Merlin said, "but insist that he fight
only with spears, for he would surely be slain in a sword-fight."

Arthur told Gryflet to kneel before him. "I cannot refuse your request," he said, and touched the young squire with his sword to make him a knight.

And then Arthur said, "Now that I have given you the gift of knighthood, I ask something from you."

"Whatever you wish, I will do," said Sir Gryflet.

"You must promise me that you will fight only with spears, whether you are on horseback or on foot."

"I promise this," said Sir Gryflet.

The new knight grabbed his spear and shield, mounted his horse, and rode off eagerly to do battle. As he approached the encampment by the well King Pellinore, alerted by the jingling harness, came out of the pavilion and asked him what he wanted.

"I have come to joust with you," said Gryflet bravely.

Pellinore saw how young Sir Gryflet was, and sighed loudly.

"Sir," he said, "if I were you I would turn back now. You are very young and inexperienced. I am much stronger than you and it would not be a fair contest. Do not force me to fight with you."

"You have no choice," Sir Gryflet answered. "I am a knight and I challenge you."

"Where do you come from, young sir?" asked the older knight.

"I am a knight of King Arthur's court," said Gryflet proudly, "and I demand a fight."

"On your head be it," King Pellinore sighed. Reluctantly he mounted his horse, levelled his great spear, and attacked.

The two knights, with pennants flying and shields at the ready, spurred their horses to a gallop and clashed violently together. Unfortunately for Sir Gryflet, his shield was instantly pierced by the spear of the stronger and more experienced knight, and he fell to the ground, gravely wounded.

Pellinore looked sadly at the fallen young man. He took off Gryflet's helmet and saw that he was badly wounded. Lifting Gryflet up in his arms he put him back on his horse. "He is a brave young knight," he said to himself sadly, "and if his life can be saved he will one day prove himself."

Then he pointed the horse in the direction from which it had come and sent it back to Camelot. The horse carried the bleeding Gryflet into the Great Hall where Arthur and knights sat at dinner.

Now Arthur, enraged by the sight of the badly wounded young knight, resolved to go alone and fight the stranger. Telling no one where he was going, he left the court before daybreak the next morning to avenge Sir Gryflet's defeat. But wise Merlin, knowing Arthur well, was waiting outside the castle walls. He tried to persuade the King to turn back. He knew that Pellinore was too strong for Arthur, even though he was a skilled and wily fighter. But Arthur would not be persuaded, and when they came to the clearing where Pellinore had set up his pavilion, he challenged him at once to do battle.

The two kings rode full tilt at each other. Arthur fought bravely, but he found that what Merlin had said was true. He was soon unhorsed, and the fight continued hand-to-hand, sword against sword. After a fierce struggle, King Pellinore struck such a hard blow that Arthur's sword broke into pieces and he lay on the ground at the mercy of his opponent.

At this moment Merlin, fearing that the King was about to be killed, intervened.

"Hold your sword, Sir Knight," he cried. "Do you know who this is? If you kill him you will bring trouble to our kingdom. The whole country will become lawless again, and everyone will fear for their lives."

"Why, who is he?" asked Pellinore.

"He is King Arthur," Merlin replied.

King Pellinore was more afraid of Arthur's anger than he was sorry at having overcome him in fair fight. He raised his sword to kill his opponent. But Merlin, seeing what he was about to do, used his mystic powers to put the warrior King into a deep sleep.

Arthur was quickly on his feet again and saw that Pellinore lay before him on the ground.

"Merlin!" he cried, "see what you have done. You have slain this brave knight with your magic powers. I would rather have lost all my possessions than have him die in this way."

"Have no fear," Merlin replied. "He is not dead but in a deep sleep from which he will awake in a few hours. If I had not cast a spell on him, you would certainly have been slain."

As it was, Arthur had been badly wounded in the conflict, so Merlin took him to a hermitage deep in the forest. There a learned healer dressed Arthur's wounds, treating them with potions made of special herbs. For three days Arthur rested until he was fit and well again. Then he and Merlin rode off together through wild and desolate countryside without pathways of any kind. There was no sign of man or beast, only rocks and stones and an ever-present mist. No birds sang, and the vegetation was brown and sparse. Arthur became increasingly alarmed. In the battle with King Pellinore his sword had been shattered and he was now unarmed.

"Merlin," he asked, "why have you brought me to this ancient and evil place? I cannot defend myself without a sword."

"It is for that reason I have brought you here," Merlin replied.

Then Arthur saw through the writhing mists that they were coming to a broad lake. Rushes and sedges grew on the margin, and tiny wavelets gently lapped against the shore.

"My lord," said Merlin, "this place is called Avalon. You will come here once more before you die."

Then he pointed across the glittering surface of the lake. "And that is the sword that will be yours."

In the center of the lake Arthur saw an arm stretching above the water, clasping a splendid sword in its hand. And then a lady of wonderful beauty came towards them, walking over the water. She was robed in green samite, and had long golden hair. In her outstretched hands she carried a jewelled scabbard.

"She is the Lady of Lake," said Merlin. "She lives below the water in a castle full of marvels. At the moment of your birth, her swordsmiths began to forge a special sword for you, called Excalibur. Ask her for that sword you see and she will give it to you."

The Lady of the Lake walked straight towards the place where Arthur and Merlin were standing on the shore. When she was near, Arthur saluted her and said, "Lady, please tell me who owns that sword that I see in the lake."

"It is for you and this is its scabbard," the Lady replied. "But there is one condition: you must swear that, before you die, you will return the sword to me."

Arthur willingly agreed. Then the Lady of the Lake showed him a small barge that was anchored close by, and told him to row out across the water and take Excalibur from the hand that held it. Arthur and Merlin tethered their horses to a tree and rowed out into the middle of the lake. When they looked back towards the shore, the Lady of the Lake had disappeared, and as soon as Arthur had taken the sword, the arm sank quickly below the surface.

The two men rowed silently back to the deserted shore and anchored the barge among the sedges. Arthur buckled the sword at his side.

"Which do you like best, the sword or its scabbard?" asked Merlin as they mounted their horses.

"The sword!" Arthur replied.

"That is an unwise choice," said Merlin. "For although Excalibur is a wonderful sword and you will win many battles with it, the scabbard is worth ten times more than the blade it sheaths. While you wear the scabbard, however badly you are wounded, you will never lose any blood. Guard the scabbard well, and always wear it when you fight."

Arthur and Merlin set off from Avalon to return to Camelot. They had no more adventures, and reached the court safely. The faithful knights were overjoyed to see their young King again, and were amazed that he had ventured alone on such a dangerous quest. But they all admired him for his bravery, and were glad they had a king who would risk his life as the other knights did.

In future years, Arthur often recounted the story of the Lady of the Lake, and how he came by the sword called Excalibur.

THE ROUND TABLE

WHEN ARTHUR reached the age of twenty-five, his thoughts turned to marriage. He asked Merlin for advice. "The wars have ended and the land is at peace. Is it not time that I found myself a wife?"

Merlin knew that Arthur, while journeying back to Camelot from his last victorious campaign, had passed through the Kingdom of Cameliarde, which was ruled by his great friend King Leodegraunce. While Arthur rested there, he had met and fallen instantly in love with King Leodegraunce's beautiful daughter Guinevere.

However, Merlin could see far into the future and feared what was going to happen. So, dreading the reply, he said to Arthur, "My lord King, it is right that a man of your nobility should marry. A king needs a queen and all your knights and barons look forward to the day of your wedding. Tell me frankly, is there a princess that you love more than any other?"

Arthur replied eagerly, "Yes, I love the daughter of King Leodegraunce, Guinevere, the fairest princess in all Britain!"

"There is no doubt of her great beauty, my lord. But I wish with all my heart that you did not love her," said Merlin sadly. For he already knew that Guinevere would not be true. He knew that her passion for one of Arthur's favorite knights would cause great trouble, and that the marriage would end in the destruction of Arthur's kingdom. But he also knew that the King's mind was made up, and so he journeyed to the court of King Leodegraunce.

Merlin told the King of Arthur's love for his daughter, and conveyed the royal request to marry Guinevere and make her Queen of England. Leodegraunce was overjoyed at the news. Arthur's fame had spread throughout the country and everyone thought he was a brave and honorable king. He immediately consented to the wedding.

Part of Merlin's mission was to negotiate the marriage dowry, as was the custom then. But King Leodegraunce, determined to please Arthur, said, "In my court there is a great round table that is made from the wood of all the different kinds of trees in Britain. It was given to me by Arthur's father, Uther Pendragon, many years ago. One hundred and fifty knights can be seated around it. I will give this round table to Arthur as my daughter's dowry, and with it one hundred knights. At the Feast of Pentecost I will bring my daughter to Camelot."

The Round Table was put into a barge, and Merlin returned to court, accompanied by the hundred knights. Arthur was delighted when he heard that his offer of marriage had been accepted. When he saw the dowry that his old friend had chosen he called all his knights together and said, "From now on you will be called the

Knights of the Round Table. Each knight will have a seat at the Round Table, and on the back of each seat the name of the knight will be written in gold letters. When a new knight is made his name too will appear. In this way, the names of the Knights of the Round Table will live for ever."

The knights sat down around the table, and saw that, because it was round, no one could complain that he was seated at the lowest end.

Then arrangements were made for the King's wedding, and messengers were sent throughout the land to tell the people of Arthur's impending marriage. And the King also sent out a declaration, saying that if any man had a favor to ask, he should come to court on the day of the wedding and ask it, and if it were not too unreasonable it would be granted.

Many people took advantage of the King's offer, and Arthur kept his word faithfully and gave them what they asked. One of those who came into the Great Hall with a request was Gawain, Arthur's favorite nephew and the eldest son of King Lot and Queen Margawse of Orkney.

"What favor do you ask of me?" asked the King kindly.

"I ask that you make me a knight," replied Gawain.

"I will gladly do so," said Arthur. "You are my sister's eldest son and I owe you that honor."

Just as Arthur thought that everyone who had come to make a request had been dealt with, a poor cowherd came into the hall, bringing with him a fair young man riding a skinny mare. The young man was tall and strong and handsome, and though he was dressed in rags, he carried himself as if he was someone of distinction.

The cowherd made his way to the King and bowed humbly before him. "Sir," he said, "I have heard that on the day of your wedding you will give any man whatever gift he asks, provided that it is not unreasonable. I have come to ask a favor."

"You have heard correctly," Arthur replied, "and I will keep my word if it is possible. What is your request?"

"I ask that this young man, my foster son, be made a knight."

The King was dismayed. It was one of the rules of knighthood that only a man of good parentage could be made a knight. But yet he felt that he could not break his word. "This is a hard thing that you ask of me," he said.

"Yes, sir, I know that it is a difficult request. It is not for myself that I ask it, but for my foster son. I have thirteen other sons, and they will all do whatever I ask them to. This boy will not do any useful work, but spends all his time practising sword-play. His one desire is to be a knight. He is no use to me, so I have brought him to you in the hope that you will grant his desire."

The King looked at the young man curiously, wondering why the son of a poor cowherd should have a taste for knightly pursuits.

"What is your name?" he asked.

"Sir, my name is Torre."

The young man spoke well and held himself so proud and straight, that Arthur determined to grant the request and make him a knight, no matter what others said.

"Have you a sword?" he asked.

Torre drew a battered sword from the scabbard that hung at his side. Then, at Arthur's command, he knelt down at the King's feet and bowed his head. And Arthur touched him on the shoulder with the sword and said, "Rise up, Sir Torre."

Then he turned to Merlin, who was standing at his side. "Tell me, have I done well to make this poor youth a knight?"

"Yes, sir, you have done well," answered the magician, "for this young man is of noble birth. He is the son of King Pellinore of the Isles, the knight of the well with whom you fought in the forest, and was entrusted to the care of his wet nurse, the sister of this cowherd, on the death of his mother."

When Arthur heard that the father of Sir Torre was the knight who had overcome him at the well he sent for him to come to court. King Pellinore was overjoyed to find that he had such a brave and handsome son. He and Arthur settled their differences, and Pellinore took one of the seats at the Round Table.

The wedding took place in the great cathedral. The archbishop joined the hands of Arthur and Guinevere together, and before the assembled clergy pronounced them man and wife. Then Arthur and his bride stood on the steps outside the church where

everyone could see them, and the people cheered and cheered when they saw their new Queen. Guinevere, dressed in a white silk robe decorated with gold filigree and pearls, outshone everyone with her beauty.

The whole of Camelot echoed to the sounds of music and dancing as the celebrations began. A magnificent banquet had been prepared for the wedding party in the Great Hall. When all the knights had taken their seats at the Round Table, three places still remained empty.

"One is for Lancelot of the Lake," Merlin explained. "He will be with you at the next Feast of Pentecost. The second is for Sir Percival, who is not yet born. As for the last place, that is the Siege Perilous, a dangerous seat. It is intended for the most noble knight of all, and if anyone else dares to take his place, then he will die."

A hush fell over those present as Merlin spoke these words, but then, remembering the joyous occasion for which they were all gathered, Arthur gave a signal for the feasting to begin.

No one had ever seen such a magnificent banquet: there was roast boar and game birds; dressed carp and dishes of fresh oysters; exotic puddings and platters of fruit from faraway places. The wine flowed freely – and then, as sometimes happens, there was a lull in the merrymaking. The noise and tumult faded quite suddenly. As silence fell Merlin rose to his feet and announced to the attentive guests, "Today begins the First Quest. There will be many other strange adventures in the future, but this will be a noble and virtuous test of chivalry. Listen!"

As he spoke, everyone heard the sound of hooves clattering on the flagstones outside. Then suddenly, a pure white hind bounded into the banqueting hall, closely pursued by a white brachet, a small hunting dog. The brachet in turn was being chased by a great pack of baying, black hounds. Round and round the sweating beasts careered, the hind trembling with sheer terror as the brachet snapped at her hindquarters. With a single despairing leap, she cleared the table, bounded once, twice, and disappeared from the hall as suddenly as she had entered it. The brachet attempted to follow, and in doing so crashed into Sir Abellus, knocking him violently sideways. He seized the dog, and clasping it firmly, strode out of the hall. By then, the black hounds were just a sound in the distance as they chased the white hind through the forest.

As the astounded guests and knights were recovering from the confusion, a fair young girl, mounted on a white palfrey, rode daintily into the hall. She reined her horse to a standstill in front of King Arthur, "My Lord King," she cried, "that cruel knight has robbed me of my sweet white hound!"

But even before the King could respond, a knight in black armor riding a huge black horse cantered into the hall. Reaching down, he seized the terrified girl and holding her firmly across his saddle, rode away as swiftly as he had arrived.

King Arthur jumped to his feet. He was uncertain what to do, as this was his wedding day. Merlin spoke for him, "Today, Sir Gawain and Sir Torre joined the Knights of the Round Table. In this First Quest, Sir Torre will find Sir Abellus and

54

bring him back here together with the white brachet he has stolen. Sir Gawain will search for the white hind. And you, King Pellinore, will bring back that fair maid and the knight who abducted her."

The three knights lost no time. They armed themselves, and rode away from Camelot.

Sir Gawain had chosen his younger brother Gaheris to be his squire, and together the two rode at speed through the forest, following the trail the white hind and the pursuing black hounds had left.

Before very long, as they rode out of the forest, they heard the sound of hounds baying. Then from the banks of a wide river they saw the white hind swimming strongly, with the hounds in the water close behind. High on a hill on the other side of the river was a fine castle.

As the brothers started to cross the river, a knight rode up on the other bank. "Do not follow the white hind unless you want to fight me!" he shouted.

Sir Gawain was not to be deterred from his quest, and continued to cross the river. When he arrived at the other side, he struck at the hostile knight and unseated him. Then he leapt from his horse and renewed the attack on foot. After a fierce fight, he slew his opponent. The way was now clear for the two brothers to cross the unguarded drawbridge and enter the castle. Following the barking of the hounds, they came to a courtyard. To their dismay the white hind lay dead and bleeding.

At this moment, the lord of the castle appeared and flew into a towering rage when he saw the hounds milling around the hind's body. He slashed at them with his sword, killing one with each blow. "You have killed the white hind my sweet lady gave me," he wept. "I will now kill all of you without mercy." And soon, the white hind was covered over with the bodies of the dead hounds.

Sir Gawain was outraged. "Why do you slay these defenceless beasts? They only did what they were trained to do."

With a snarl, the lord of the castle turned on Gawain, and a fierce duel took place across the courtyard, first one way and then the other. Sir Gawain was the better fighter, and soon his attacker was begging for mercy.

"Why should you have mercy, when you showed none!" Gawain raised his sword, preparing to strike the final blow.

Suddenly, the lady of the castle, who had been watching the duel from her chamber, ran forward sobbing wretchedly and threw herself over the defeated knight to shield him. At the same time Sir Gawain, unable to stop the blow, brought his sword down and struck off her head instead of his enemy's.

Gawain was horrified at this terrible accident. Filled with remorse, he allowed the knight to rise unhurt. "Your life is spared," he said. "Who are you anyway?"

"I am Blamore of the Marsh, and I wish that you would kill me now, for I have lost everything that I ever loved!"

Gawain replied, "Go now to Camelot and tell King Arthur truthfully what has happened here, and that Sir Gawain, the son of King Lot of Orkney whose mother is Margawse, the sister of King Arthur, has sent you."

No sooner had the sad Sir Blamore departed, when four knights rushed forward and attacked Sir Gawain and Gaheris and wounded both of them severely before throwing them into the dungeons. And they might have remained there if four fair ladies of the castle had not begged for their lives. When their captors learned that the prisoners were from King Arthur's court they were released, for these knights too were loyal to King Arthur. When they heard why Sir Gawain had sought the white hind, they severed its head and tied it to Gawain's saddle to prove that he had succeeded in the quest. But they also commanded him to carry the dead lady's body before him on the saddle, and they attached her head with a rope to his neck.

Sir Gawain and his brother Gaheris returned sadly to Camelot. Arthur and Guinevere were distressed by the unchivalrous behavior of their knight. "From now on, Sir Gawain," said the Queen sternly, "you must be the champion of all women, whatever their birth." And Sir Gawain swore that he would always be the most courteous and chivalrous knight.

Sir Torre's adventure started the following morning when he rode off in search of the knight who had stolen the brachet. As he reached a clearing in the forest he heard a rustle in the bushes. A fierce dwarf armed with a stave sprang forward and hit Sir Torre's horse hard across the nose, causing the poor beast great pain.

Sir Torre was very angry at this unprovoked attack. "Why did you strike my horse, dwarf?" he asked.

"You will go no further until you joust with the two knights I serve," the dwarf snarled.

Sir Torre wanted none of this. "I will not wait, for I come from Camelot on a quest to find a knight that has stolen a white brachet."

The dwarf did not listen. He blew a loud note on the horn that hung from his girdle and immediately two heavily armed knights appeared, their lances at the ready. Sir Torre turned swiftly, for he had scarcely enough time to ready his own lance, and rode at the first knight. Using all his strength he unhorsed his opponent in a single pass, and dealt with the second knight in the same way.

Sir Torre stood over the defeated knights as they lay on the ground. "Go to the court of King Arthur," he said sternly, "and say that Sir Torre has sent you, or else I will slay both of you now!"

Both knights swore to obey him and got ready to leave. Sir Torre felt something tugging at his foot, and when he looked down he saw the dwarf. "Let me be your squire," he begged, "for I will no longer serve such cowardly knights as those two." Sir Torre agreed, and the two rode off together.

When they had gone some distance, the dwarf said, "I will lead you to the white brachet that you are looking for."

They continued through the forest until they came to an encampment beside an old abbey. The dwarf rode straight towards two silken pavilions, one white and the other red. Sir Torre dismounted and entered the red pavilion. A girl lay asleep and beside her was the white brachet. The dog ran to him and he picked it up. But as he strode from the pavilion, the girl woke up and cried out, "Stop thief, you have taken my dog!"

Sir Torre was about to get on his horse when Sir Abellus appeared mounted. He was armed and ready to charge, and shouted at the top of his voice, "Return the brachet you have stolen from my lady at once."

Sir Torre had no intention of doing this, so he mounted rapidly and took his lance from the dwarf. The two knights rode at each other again and again, until Sir Torre delivered a heavy blow that toppled his opponent. But still the fallen knight refused to yield. As Sir Torre stood over him, a lady on a palfrey rode out from the forest, and

cried, "Sir Knight, in all justice you must cut off Sir Abellus's head, for not two hours ago, he slew my brother although I begged and begged for mercy."

Sir Abellus could not deny it, and as his guilt was plain, Sir Torre did as the lady had asked. She invited him to accompany her to her aged husband's castle, where he was made very welcome.

The following morning, Sir Torre returned to Camelot and told the court of his adventures. King Arthur and his Queen were very proud of their new knight, who had proved himself a worthy son of the valiant King Pellinore.

King Pellinore left Camelot on his quest to find the abducted maid and the Black Knight. On the way he came on a weeping lady nursing a badly wounded knight.

"Help me, help me, for my lord is dying!" the lady cried.

But Pellinore was so single-minded about his quest that he would not stop. He rode on through the forest until he heard the familiar sound of sword-fighting not far off. As he drew near, Pellinore peered through the trees and was surprised to see that one of the combatants was the Black Knight. The other knight was dressed in bright green armor, which reflected the light that streamed through the trees surrounding the little glade. Both knights were wounded, and their blood stained the grassy ground. The fair maid crouched at the side, sheltered by a bush.

"Why are you fighting?" King Pellinore asked the knights.

"I am Sir Meliot of Logure," the Green Knight replied. "This is Lady Nimue, my cousin, and I am defending her honor against this disreputable knight."

The Black Knight, taking advantage of the situation, leapt forward and killed King Pellinore's horse. Then he turned savagely on the newcomer, but Pellinore, outraged, felled him with a single blow to the head, splitting his black helmet to the chin.

Sir Meliot mounted his horse. "Please accompany my cousin, Lady Nimue, back to King Arthur's court," he said to Pellinore, "and one day, you shall see me there too."

King Pellinore mounted the Black Knight's horse, and he and Lady Nimue rode slowly back through the forest. As they passed the well Pellinore saw to his horror that the anguished lady and her knight were both dead: he of his wounds, and she in her grief by her own hand. Lady Nimue, when she found out what had happened, advised Pellinore to take the bodies back to Camelot to be honorably buried.

When Pellinore told what had happened Queen Guinevere reproached him for his lack of chivalry. "You could have saved the life of the lady beside the well," she said.

Then Merlin took Pellinore aside and revealed to him that the lady he had refused to help was his own daughter Alyne, who had married the good knight Sir Miles of Landys, and was the half-sister of Sir Torre. King Pellinore, who had never known his daughter, but had searched for her for many years, was inconsolable. He, like Sir Gawain, was a changed man from that day forward.

THE FALSE EXCALIBUR

ARTHUR'S MARRIAGE to Guinevere made him even more popular with his people. Whenever the King and Queen travelled about the kingdom they were greeted with warmth and affection, for Arthur had gained a reputation for being a brave and just ruler, and Guinevere charmed everyone with her infectious gaiety. It would surely not be long before Arthur had an heir.

Peace now reigned in most parts of Britain – even the northern lords had stopped causing trouble, and Arthur no longer lay awake at night wondering whether he had the right to be King. His knights rode out daily to put right injustices and prove themselves on dangerous quests. It was a time of unity at Camelot.

The Lady of the Lake, who had given Arthur his magic sword Excalibur, seemed to have taken the King under her special protection. Often in the course of his life she came to his assistance, to save him from danger and death. And Arthur was shortly to find himself in a dangerous situation where he would be needing the help of the mysterious lady who lived beneath the waters of the lake.

Morgan le Fay could not bear the loyalty and love the people of Britain showed to Arthur, especially after he had married the beautiful Guinevere and founded the Order of the Round Table. She was still consumed with hatred for her half-brother and continually looked for ways to destroy him in order to avenge her father's death.

This evil enchantress was the most beautiful woman in the land, and many kings and powerful knights courted her and sought her hand in marriage. Eventually she married King Urygens of Gore, a fine handsome man, who was devoted to her and as yet completely unaware of her sorcery. She had also seduced a French knight called Accolon of Gaul, who was besotted with love for her. The wicked Queen thought that if she could only kill Arthur and her husband, she could marry Accolon and make him king of both their lands.

As part of her evil plot to bring about Arthur's downfall Morgan le Fay changed herself into the shape of an ugly dwarf. In the workshops below her castle, she fashioned an exact replica of Arthur's magic sword. The false Excalibur and its lustrous scabbard were both perfect in every detail. Now all that remained was to make the exchange with an unsuspecting Arthur.

One spring morning Arthur, King Urygens and Sir Accolon went hunting in the mysterious forests that then covered South Wales. Now that Arthur's reign had brought a time of peace to Britain, following the chase was one of the greatest entertainments for the knights of the court. For apart from occasional tournaments and quests, there was little else to occupy their time. At least while they hunted, their horsemanship remained keen; and when they were successful, the great spits in the kitchens were loaded with fresh meat.

In the excitement of the chase the three men became separated from the other huntsmen. They sighted a great hart, and followed the beast many miles, galloping fast and furiously through the forest. As they were about to close up on the hart, their mounts became too exhausted to continue the chase and they were forced to rest.

They had stopped just at the edge of the forest, and there on a grassy slope they saw the exhausted hart falter, then fall to the ground and die.

"Well," said Arthur, "it is too late for us to find the other knights. We will look for lodgings for the night."

The three knights dismounted, and discovered that the grassy slope led to the bank of a great stretch of water. As they walked through the gathering darkness towards the shore, a small ship richly hung with many-colored silks and lit up with a dazzling array of lights glided towards them and came to rest silently against the bank.

Twelve beautiful maidens dressed in white samite appeared on deck and without uttering a word, gestured to the huntsmen to come on board. Silently they served the hunters with as much food and wine as they wanted, while sweet music played, and strange perfumes scented the air. When they had eaten their fill, each man was led separately to a sumptuously furnished cabin, and before very long all three were overcome with sleep.

When Arthur woke from his dreamless sleep, he found himself in a cold, damp dungeon, shackled hand and foot with heavy chains. As his eyes became accustomed to the gloom, he saw twenty other knights, all shackled as he was.

"Who holds you captive here?" asked Arthur.

"The lord of the castle is an evil man called Sir Damas," said a frail, bearded man dressed in rags. "Some of us have been imprisoned here for more than eight years."

"Damas took the castle from his elder brother, the noble knight Sir Outlake, who now lives in a small manor. Outlake is much loved by the local people, and has offered to fight in single combat against his brother to regain his inheritance. But Sir Damas is too cowardly to accept the challenge."

As one of the other knights was explaining this, a maid carrying a lamp came into the dungeon, and spoke to King Arthur. "Sir, you can regain your liberty, and that of all the other knights, if you will fight in single combat for my lord."

Arthur was uncertain at first how he should reply. His imprisoned companions had warned him that they too had all been asked the same question, and all of them had refused. So Arthur said, "Your lord is an evil and cowardly knight and I would never fight in his defense. But I would rather die than remain any longer in this foul and damp prison!"

"I will arrange everything," the maid said quickly, and turned to go.

But Arthur stopped her. "Wait, surely I have seen you before at Camelot?"

"I am Sir Damas's daughter and have never been there in my life."

The girl lied, for Arthur had recognized her as one of Morgan le Fay's serving maids. He began to feel uneasy, and wondered what had happened to his fellow huntsmen.

Meanwhile, King Urygens woke to find himself in his own bed beside his sleeping wife, Morgan le Fay. She did not answer his puzzled questions. Although he was beginning to suspect her sorcery, her magic powers were so powerful that the noble knight was quite unable to persist with his questioning, and soon fell asleep again. Morgan smiled a deep mysterious smile, for her evil plans were beginning to take effect.

Sir Accolon of Gaul also slept a dreamless sleep, and eventually woke to find himself in a green meadow, precariously balanced on the stone parapet of a deep well. If he had moved in his sleep he would certainly have fallen to his death. Hastily he stepped down beside the well. Accolon wondered what had become of his companions, and swore that he would slay all women who dealt in black magic.

Just then an extremely ugly dwarf approached, carrying a magnificent sword and scabbard. The dwarf saluted the knight and said gruffly, "My mistress, Morgan le Fay, because her lord is dead, asks that for her sake you fight today with a strange knight. As a token of her great love for you, she sends you this sword. I am also instructed to tell you that you must be certain to wear the scabbard when you fight so that no harm will come to you."

The dwarf handed Excalibur and its brilliant scabbard to Sir Accolon. For while King Arthur lay in his bewitched sleep, one of Morgan le Fay's serving maids had crept into the cabin and stolen Excalibur from him.

"I will certainly be Morgan le Fay's champion!" the bedazzled knight replied warmly. Sir Accolon was enraptured by the task his lady had set him: here was a chance to impress her with his bravery and skill. He followed the dwarf to Sir Outlake's manor. This noble knight had been wounded in the thigh by a spear thrust, and he lay on a litter protected by six squires. He had just heard that Sir Damas had found a champion, and was furious that he was unable to fight. Sir Accolon immediately offered to fight in his place. The squires brought him some armor and a warhorse, and led him away to the appointed place.

Meanwhile, the six squires of Sir Damas had armed and mounted King Arthur. Just as they were leading him out of the castle gate, the maiden whom Arthur had last seen in the castle dungeon rode up on a white palfrey carrying a sword and its scabbard.

"Your sister, Morgan le Fay, has learned of your danger and asked me to bring you your sword Excalibur," she said. "The Queen sends you her regards and wishes you good fortune in this contest."

When he heard these kind words Arthur forgot whatever worries he had felt about his sister. "I knew that you were one of Morgan le Fay's waiting women," he said as he buckled on the sword. "Tell your mistress I send my thanks and we will celebrate my victory when I return."

Arthur rode towards the field of battle feeling lighthearted and confident: he knew that with his own sword and its magic scabbard he could not lose blood if he were wounded. Not for one moment did he suspect the treachery of Morgan le Fay.

The two knights, both armored from head to toe and with their visors closed, prepared to fight. Neither knew the true identity of the other because their shields were without crests. A crowd had gathered in the little meadow to watch the encounter, for they hated Sir Damas as much as they esteemed Sir Outlake. Serfs stood shoulder to shoulder with knights around the edge of the field, waiting for the single blast on a horn that would signal the start of the fight.

The coarse note of the horn rang out and the two knights galloped full tilt at each other. They clashed so violently that both were unhorsed at the first pass. As the terrible but unequal sword-fight began, the Lady of the Lake rode up to the scene of combat. Through her magic powers she knew of Morgan le Fay's murderous intentions and had sensed that Arthur was in great danger.

She realized at once that Arthur's sword was useless and Sir Accolon seemed to be invincible. Though both knights struck with equal force Arthur's sword made no impression on Sir Accolon's armor, whereas his opponent drew blood with every stroke. Soon the little green meadow was stained red with Arthur's blood.

Sir Accolon, scenting victory, redoubled his attack. Again and again he struck at Arthur, and the watching crowd marvelled that the wounded knight could still stand and fight. At last, the false Excalibur broke in two pieces.

"Yield, Sir Knight," Accolon jeered, "or I will slice your head off with my sword!" He slashed at Arthur again, who could only defend himself with his shield.

At that point the Lady of the Lake cast a spell that caused Sir Accolon's scabbard to come loose, for she saw Arthur was lost without her help. She caught it as it fell to the ground and called to Arthur to buckle it to his waist. And Sir Accolon did not complete his mighty sword stroke either, because Excalibur dropped from his hands to the ground.

Arthur grabbed the sword and knew at once it was his own Excalibur. He turned on Sir Accolon and cried, "Sir Knight, it is your turn to die! Now that I have my own sword, I will repay you for all the blood I have lost and the pain of my wounds!" He leapt forward and struck Sir Accolon, who fell mortally wounded at his feet.

"Kill me, for I will never yield," said the dying knight. "It will be a noble death, for you are the best knight I have ever fought."

Arthur lowered his sword quickly. He was beginning to suspect the truth. "Tell me from what land you have come," he said, "for you are a brave and honorable knight."

"Sir Knight, I come from the royal court of King Arthur, and I am called Accolon of Gaul."

"But who gave you the sword?" asked Arthur, surprised.

Sir Accolon could only reply sadly, "Queen Morgan le Fay gave it to me and entreated me to be her champion. She told me that her husband King Urygens was dead, and that I would be king in his place if I won this battle. And who are you?"

Arthur pulled up his visor, and leaning over the dying knight, said, "Do you not recognize your King?"

Then Accolon cried out, "Lord King, have mercy! I did not know it was you!"

"My sister Morgan le Fay is to blame for this," said Arthur furiously. "Merlin has warned me about her, but I thought that she had overcome her hatred of me. If she could do this to me, I can believe what she has done to you and forgive your treachery."

Arthur was very weak from loss of blood, so the attending squires carried him and Sir Accolon to a nearby abbey. There the wounds of the two knights were attended to by the abbess and her nuns. Arthur recovered rapidly, but nothing could be done to save Sir Accolon, who died the next morning.

The King ordered that Accolon's body should be put on a bier and taken to his sister Morgan le Fay. A solemn procession, headed by the Lady of the Lake on horseback and escorted by six knights, entered Surhaute. When Morgan le Fay realized that her plot had failed she rode straight to the abbey where Arthur still rested, with the intention of stealing Excalibur. She knew that while he possessed Excalibur and its magic sheath, he was safe against her sorcery.

She asked the nuns how her brother was, and they, not knowing that she had come to do him injury, told her that he was sleeping.

"Do not wake him, then," she said. "I will go and look at him as he lies asleep." And she went very quietly into the chamber where Arthur lay sleeping, hoping to steal his sword.

But even in his sleep, Arthur lay with one hand firmly grasping the sword. Morgan le Fay dared not steal Excalibur for fear of waking him, but the scabbard lay nearby on a wooden chair. Concealing it under her cloak, she rode hastily away from the abbey.

When Arthur woke up he saw at once that the scabbard was missing. When the nuns told him that Morgan le Fay had been to his chamber he leapt from his bed, ill though he was, and called for two of the knights to come with him.

They rode at breakneck speed through the night, following the fresh tracks that were clearly visible in the moonlight. Very soon they caught sight of her, and since their horses were fresher than hers, Morgan le Fay realized that there was no chance of escape.

"But whatever becomes of me, my brother shall not have this scabbard," she said to herself.

Seeing a lake just in front of her, she galloped towards it and flung the scabbard far out into the deepest part. Morgan le Fay then used her magic powers to turn herself and her followers into stones that matched the boulders strewn around the valley, so that when King Arthur and the knights rode up a few moments later, there was no one to be seen. Arthur searched in vain for the scabbard before riding back to the abbey.

As soon as they were gone, Morgan le Fay changed herself into her own form again and hurried back to her own castle. There she started to plan another evil scheme by which she might kill her half-brother.

When Arthur returned to Camelot after his fight with Sir Accolon everyone rejoiced that he had managed to escape from the terrible danger that had threatened his life. But back in the security of her own castle Morgan le Fay was again using her magical powers to try to destroy her brother. She made a wonderful cloak, fit for a king to wear, and chose an innocent young maid from her household to take it to Arthur.

"Go to the court at Camelot," she instructed the maid, "and tell the King that I am sorry for the wicked things I have done in the past and want with all my heart to make peace with him. Say that I ask his forgiveness, and have sent him this magnificent cloak as a gift. Take it, but do not under any circumstances wear it yourself."

The maid was puzzled by her mistress's request, but promised to do as she was told. Then, carrying the cloak in a basket, she rode off for Camelot, which was several days' journey away. She arrived in the evening, when the King and Queen Guinevere were dining in the Great Hall, together with the whole company of knights.

The maid bowed low before King Arthur and said, "My lord King, I have come from my mistress Queen Morgan le Fay. She has sent me to beg your pardon for all the

harm that she has done to you. She swears that she will never again attempt to hurt you and now she wants more than anything else to make peace with you. As a token of her respect and love for you, she sends you this magnificent cloak. It is a magic cloak, and it protects anyone who wears it from all evil!"

When the maid spread out the cloak everyone was astonished by its beauty and richness. Never before had they seen such colors, so many wonderful patterns. Even King Arthur, who at first did not want to hear the message from his sister, began to believe that maybe there could at last be peace between them.

He smiled at the girl and said, "I will gladly accept this splendid gift. When you return to my sister, tell her that she is now welcome at Camelot!"

"My mistress asked that you should wear the cloak so that I can tell her how well it suited you," the girl replied timidly.

"Certainly I will!"

King Arthur rose to take the cloak from the maid but Lady Nimue, who was seated nearby, whispered urgently in his ear, "Do not be deceived. It is sure to be a trap. The cloak is evil and should never have been allowed into the castle if it has been woven by the magic of Morgan le Fay. We must find out what magic it possesses. Ask the maid to wear it first!"

"Let the maid wear the cloak," agreed Merlin.

"I cannot," protested the terrified girl. "My mistress made me swear never to wear the cloak under any circumstances. I dare not disobey her."

But Merlin insisted, "Nevertheless, wear it you shall!" He moved towards her with the cloak coiled around his staff, for he would not touch it.

The trembling girl took the cloak from the magician, put it around her slender shoulders, and fastened its clasp nervously. "Please do not tell my mistress that I wore the cloak," she begged.

At that very moment, there was a flash and the cloak burst into fierce flames, completely engulfing the poor girl. In no time at all, there were was nothing left of the cloak and its wearer but a small heap of black ashes.

Arthur was filled with horror at what he had just seen. "My sister is pitiless!" he cried. "A poor innocent girl has been sacrificed in her efforts to kill me. Will there be no end to this treachery?"

But once more Queen Morgan le Fay's wicked plans had failed, and from that moment on King Arthur swore that he would never trust his sister again.

MERLIN DEPARTS

MANY STORIES were told of the King's gentle and forgiving nature. But for the presence of Merlin, Arthur would never have survived the constant attempts to bring about his downfall. He had grown used to the presence of the wise magician, and relied on his advice to survive many perilous adventures. But now the old man knew that his own time at Camelot was coming to an end, and because he could see into the future, he knew exactly what his fate would be. When Merlin told Arthur what was to happen, the King found what he heard very difficult to believe.

"Why, with all your wisdom, can you not avoid these fateful events that you prophesy?" he asked.

"Wisdom by itself is not enough," Merlin replied gravely, "as you will surely find out. Much as you will miss my advice to you over little matters, there will come a time when you would give up your throne to have me at your side again."

Merlin went on to prophesy many things that would happen in the future, and warned Arthur of the enemies he would meet. But the magician knew that although he might tell Arthur exactly what the future held for Camelot, there was nothing the King or anyone else could do to change it.

Lady Nimue had been brought to court by King Pellinore at the end of the First Quest and Merlin, who had always been so cautious and wise in other matters, had fallen hopelessly in love with her. He wanted nothing more than to spend every hour with her, but he knew there would be a high price to pay for his passion.

Merlin pursued Lady Nimue ardently and sought her company with the determination of a boy experiencing his first love. Wherever she went, he followed, and together they travelled to many faraway places.

At the foreign courts they visited Merlin used his powers of prophecy to help and guide other rulers that they met. But eventually Lady Nimue became bored, and found Merlin's constant demands for her love embarrassing.

She started to question Merlin about his magic powers, and he taught her everything she wanted to know in the hope that she would love him in return. But Lady Nimue was crafty and successfully resisted his advances. Soon she had learned nearly all of Merlin's magic, and she was ready to play the role that fate had cast for her. But first she had to make sure that the old magician could not use his wizardry to foil her. If he truly wanted to possess her, she decreed, he must first swear not to use any magic to achieve his wish.

Merlin, completely enslaved but also perfectly aware of what was to happen, swore a binding oath that he would not do so. However, even as he promised, Merlin

did not forget his affection and duty towards Arthur, and demanded that she too must swear an oath to protect the King. This Nimue gladly did, for now she was ready to cast the final spell over Merlin.

Knowing that the time had come for him to leave Camelot, Merlin said goodbye to Arthur, and rode away from court for the last time. As they were riding through a leafy glade in the forest Merlin felt an overwhelming and strange tiredness. He lay down under the shade of a hawthorn in full blossom, and fell into a deep sleep.

When he awoke, it was as people do in a dream and his senses were filled with the sounds and scents of the forest. Nimue took him by the hand and led him gently towards the Vale of Avalon, their horses following behind. And there they came to the shore where years before Merlin and King Arthur had received the sword Excalibur from the Lady of the Lake. As they approached, the waters parted, revealing a flight of stone steps.

Merlin docilely followed Lady Nimue to a dark cavern deep beneath the lake. Then as he passed by her, she kissed him on the forehead, and with a wave of her hand caused a mighty boulder to roll forward. Merlin lay down on the cold stone floor of the cavern as the boulder rolled across its entrance, and the waters of the lake closed to hide it for ever.

Lady Nimue mounted her horse and rode away, and Merlin even now lies sleeping in the underground cavern.

On the day before the Feast of Pentecost, one year after his marriage to Guinevere, King Arthur and some of his knights rode out early from Camelot to hunt in the forest. They had not gone far when they met four squires carrying a wounded knight on a litter. The man was groaning with pain, and when Arthur rode over to see if he could help, he saw that there was a broken sword blade sticking out of a gaping wound in his side.

"Tell me, Sir Knight," said Arthur solicitously, "how you came by this wound, and how we may help you?"

Not realizing who he was speaking to, the wounded man replied, "I am on my way to the court of King Arthur. I have been told by the Lady of the Lake that a man who can heal my wound is arriving there on the Feast of Pentecost."

The knight fell back on to the litter, exhausted with the effort of speaking. But his words had intrigued the King, and he returned at once to Camelot, eager to see if the mysterious visitor had arrived.

Next morning, when all the knights were gathered at the Round Table, a trumpet call sounded and into the Great Hall rode the Lady of the Lake. Behind her came a fine young man – a squire who looked of an age to be knighted. He was tall and broad-shouldered, every inch a warrior, but his face was gentle and open.

"I come to you, my lord King," said the Lady of the Lake, "to bring my foster child, Lancelot, the son of King Ban and Queen Elaine of Benoic in France. It was Merlin's last wish that he should come to your court at Pentecost and be made a knight."

Just then the wounded knight from the forest arrived at the castle and was carried by his squires into the Hall. When he saw Lancelot beside the Lady of the Lake he called out to him, "Help me, young sir, help me. Your hands alone can heal me."

Lancelot walked over to the litter where the man lay and knelt down beside him. Very gently he removed the broken sword blade, and as soon as it was pulled out the wound was miraculously healed.

Astonished by this miracle, the knights listened attentively as the Lady of the Lake told the court how Lancelot had been brought up beneath the magic waters of the lake at Avalon, and how she had taught him all the knightly skills and the code of chivalry by which a knight should live.

"He is indeed a true-born knight," agreed King Arthur, and reaching for his sword Excalibur he laid it on Lancelot's shoulder. "Arise, Sir Lancelot," he said.

Lancelot took his place at the Round Table and was soon one of Arthur's most loved and trusted knights. He served the King loyally and rode out on many adventures. But all the quests he undertook, and all the great battles he fought, were for Queen Guinevere's sake. When his opponents yielded to him in battle, he sent them to swear allegiance to the Queen in return for sparing their lives. When he won prizes in the tournaments in which he jousted, he gave them all to Guinevere. He was willing to fight for her honor against any knight in the world. For Lancelot had fallen in love with Guinevere, and knew that he could love no other woman.

Sir Lancelot
of the Lake

O NE DAY, Sir Lancelot and his cousin Sir Lionel rode out from Camelot in search of adventures that would test their knightly skills. It was a hot day and both knights were fully armed. By the middle of the afternoon Lancelot was overwhelmed with a desire to sleep, and he lay down in the shade of an apple tree.

While Lancelot slept, Lionel sat nearby guarding their horses. Suddenly three knights rode out of the forest pursued by a fourth knight on a powerful warhorse. Sir Lionel got to his feet in order to see them better, and watched the fourth knight catch up with the three in front and overcome them one by one. Then he tied them up with their own bridles and flung them face downwards across their horses' backs.

"Here is a chance to win some honor for myself," thought Lionel, "if I defeat this knight." So, taking care not to wake his sleeping cousin, he mounted his horse and rode after them.

Soon he caught up with the warrior knight and challenged him to defend himself. The knight turned round, set his spear in its rest, and came against Lionel so fast that he flung both horse and man to the ground. Then he dismounted, tied Sir Lionel's hands and feet, threw him over his own horse and led him away with the other three knights. When they reached his castle he took away all their armor and shut them up in a dark dungeon.

Back at Camelot, Sir Hector de Maris missed his cousins Sir Lancelot and Sir Lionel and, thinking that they must have set out in search of adventure, rode out to join them. He travelled a long way without finding any trace of them, and eventually he stopped and asked a forester whether he had seen the two knights.

The old man told Hector how he had seen several knights riding towards the home of the powerful Sir Turquin. "He lives scarcely a mile from here in a strong castle by a ford. There is a great oak tree beside the ford, and from its branches hang the shields of all the knights that he has thrown into his dungeon. You will also see a large copper basin. Strike it with your spear and Sir Turquin will come out and do battle with you."

Sir Hector thanked the forester and spurred on his horse towards the castle by the ford. Just as the old man had said, a collection of shields hung from a great tree, and among them Hector recognized that of his cousin, Sir Lionel. Angrily he struck at the copper basin until its loud clanging echoed round the castle walls, and then he turned to let his horse drink at the ford.

"Come out of the water and fight with me!" cried a loud voice behind him. Turning quickly Hector came face to face with the powerful Sir Turquin. He charged immediately and succeeded in landing a blow on the huge knight. But then Turquin charged Sir Hector, caught him under the arm and lifted him right out of the saddle on the point of his spear. In this humiliating position Hector was carried into the castle.

"What are you doing here, cousin?" said an astonished Sir Lionel as Hector was thrown down on the dungeon floor.

"I could ask the same of you," snapped Hector, who was still smarting from the humiliation of his defeat. He looked around at the other knights. "And where is Lancelot?"

"I left him sleeping under an apple tree," said Lionel bitterly.

And there Lancelot still lay, peacefully asleep, unaware of what had happened to his cousin and half-brother. While he slept, four queens came by, riding on white mules. Beside them rode four knights, who held a green silk awning on the points of their spears to shield the queens from the heat of the sun. As they passed by the apple tree Lancelot's horse neighed, and they saw the knight in armor lying on the ground.

The four queens stopped to look at the knight who lay so peacefully sleeping. Lancelot had taken off his helmet, and when the queens saw his face they knew at once who he was, because his fame had spread throughout the land. He looked so strong and handsome that all four queens immediately fell in love, and began squabbling among themselves about who would have him.

One of the queens was Morgan le Fay, King Arthur's half-sister, who was skilled in the magic arts. "We can't all have him," said the wicked Queen, "so let us not waste time quarrelling. I will put a spell on him so that he will sleep for many hours. We will carry him away to my castle, and when he wakes he can choose one of us to be his love – or else die a horrible death in my dungeons."

The other three queens agreed to this plan, so Morgan le Fay cast a spell of sleep upon him and the four knights laid him on his shield and carried him into her castle.

When Lancelot woke up at last he found himself lying on the floor in a cold stone cell. He raised himself up on one elbow and looked around, wondering where he was and how he came to be there. When a young girl unlocked the door and came in with something to eat, Lancelot begged her to tell him where he was. But she shook her head. "Sir, I can tell you nothing now," she said, and hurried out of the chamber.

That night Lancelot lay awake on the bare floor of the empty cell. There was no way of escape, for the door was locked and the windows heavily barred. All his armor and weapons had been taken away from him, so he was helpless in the hands of his captors. Nobody came near him until the next morning, and then the four queens, dressed in their richest gowns, came into his prison cell.

"Sir Knight," said Morgan le Fay, "we have brought you here because you are the most noble knight of Sir Arthur's court. We know that you have sworn to serve no other woman except Queen Guinevere, but now that you are our prisoner you must choose one of us, or stay in this prison until you die."

Lancelot raised his head proudly – if Morgan le Fay thought he would be frightened by her threat then she did not know him. "I would rather die in prison than choose one of you," he said scornfully. "I will always be true to my lady Guinevere and serve her faithfully."

"Then you refuse us?" asked Morgan le Fay, her eyes glinting vengefully.

"Yes, I refuse the lot of you!" cried Lancelot.

The four queens went away threatening terrible things and Lancelot was left alone once more, wondering what cruel death they were planning for him. He paced restlessly up and down the tiny cell until the girl arrived with his food again.

"Please," he begged her, "help me to escape, and I promise to repay you."

The girl admired Lancelot for his loyalty and bravery, and she was indignant that the queens should keep such a noble knight prisoner. She was also in need of some help herself, so she said to him softly, "I would ask you then, Sir, to fight on behalf of my father, King Bagdemagus. Another king makes war on him. They have arranged to hold a tournament on Tuesday next and whoever wins will be acclaimed the victor. They have had one tournament already, and the other king brought three knights from Arthur's court who overcame my father. I hear from my mistress that you are Sir Lancelot of the Lake, the bravest knight that ever lived, and if you will fight on my father's side, victory will surely be his in the coming battle. If you will promise to fight for my father, then I will find a way to get you out of this dungeon."

"I know your father well," Lancelot replied. "King Bagdemagus is a good king and a noble knight and I will gladly fight for him at the tournament."

Very early the next morning the girl came to the dungeon before anyone else was awake, bringing with her Lancelot's armor and weapons. Then she led the way out of the castle, opening twelve locked and bolted doors so that Lancelot could make his escape. Finding his horse in the stables, Lancelot rode off swiftly into the forest until he reached the abbey where he was to wait for King Bagdemagus to join him.

King Bagdemagus was delighted that he had such a splendid knight to fight for him, and he outlined the plans he had made for the coming battle.

"Which knights from Arthur's court fought against you in the last tournament?" asked Lancelot.

"They were Sir Agravain, Sir Mador and Sir Gahalantine," the King replied.

Lancelot was glad to hear this, for none of them were his particular friends. If they had been, he would have been sorry to fight against them. "Sir," he said to Bagdemagus, "I will certainly fight for you and do my best to gain victory. Send me three of your best and most trusted knights, and let them carry blank shields in place of

their own. I will also carry a shield that is blank, so that no one will know which knights we are. We four will wait in that little wood close to where the tournament is being held, and be ready to come to your aid as soon as you need us."

King Bagdemagus did as Lancelot suggested, and on the day of the tournament Lancelot and the three knights hid themselves in the little wood and waited for the battle to begin. They soon saw that Bagdemagus was likely to be beaten, for his enemy had twice as many knights in the field. The two sides met together in a wild charge, but Bagdemagus met with a bad reverse at the very beginning of the fight. Many of his knights were unhorsed, while only a few of the other side fell. It looked as though the battle would soon be over.

At that moment Lancelot and his three companions rode into the thick of the fight and laid about them so fiercely that many of the enemy wavered and fell. Lancelot himself felled five of them with the first stroke of his spear, and soon twelve more were overcome. Heartened by this unexpected assistance, Bagdemagus's other knights rallied, and soon things began to grow more even. The three knights from Arthur's court – Agravain, Mador and Gahalantine – did their best to unhorse Lancelot. They did not know who he was because of his blank shield, but they saw that he was far the most powerful of their opponents, and each wanted the honor of defeating him. But they could not unseat the great knight, and soon Lancelot had overcome them all.

And so, thanks to Lancelot, Bagdemagus won the victory over the enemy king and saved his kingdom from destruction.

King Bagdemagus and his daughter took Lancelot back to their castle and ordered a great feast in his honor. Lancelot rested there for the night, but the next morning, although they begged him to stay longer, he was anxious to go on his way.

"I have still to find my cousin Sir Lionel," he said. "He went away while I was asleep and I fear that he may have come to some harm."

King Bagdemagus thanked Lancelot again and again for his help, and he rode off to continue his adventures.

A few days later, as Lancelot was riding along a stream that ran through a thick patch of forest, he met Sir Turquin.

"Who dares to trespass on my land?" bellowed the huge knight.

"This lands belongs to the King, not you," Lancelot replied. "I have as much right to ride here as you have."

Sir Turquin shook with fury at the impudence of the young knight. "Defend yourself, Sir Knight," he snarled. "We will soon see who is master here."

The two knights drew apart, set their spears in the rests, and came together as fast as their horses could gallop. Each struck the other so hard in the middle of the shield that the horses dropped dead at the shock. The two knights were flung to the ground, and continued to fight on foot. For two hours they struggled fiercely, neither able to gain any advantage over the other, though both were wounded and out of breath. At last they were so exhausted that they had to pause for a while and rest.

Turquin looked at Lancelot with grudging admiration. "You are the best knight that I have ever met," he said. "I would willingly make peace with you, if you will make peace with me. Let us make a truce, and because of the splendid fight you have put up against me, I will set all my prisoners free – as long as you are not the knight who slew my brother, Sir Cardos, for on him I have sworn to take revenge."

"I slew your brother," said Lancelot calmly. "I slew Sir Cardos in a fair and honorable fight. I am Lancelot of the Lake."

When Turquin heard the name he grasped his sword again. "To the death!" he shouted, and turned on Lancelot savagely. They fought long and hard, but at last Lancelot struck a well-aimed blow and sliced off Turquin's head.

Lancelot took the keys of the castle from the dead knight's body and released all the prisoners, including his cousin Sir Lionel, Sir Hector de Maris, and King Arthur's foster brother, Sir Kay. After celebrating their new-found freedom all the knights promised to be at Camelot by next Pentecost to swear allegiance to King Arthur and Queen Guinevere.

Lancelot continued on his travels once more and came to the far reaches of Cornwall. For several days the coastline was shrouded in a thick mist, and he had to ride slowly along the clifftop path for fear of losing his footing. Eventually he saw Tintagel Castle in the distance and rode towards it eagerly, hoping to find some food and shelter for the night. As he approached the castle gates two large shapes loomed out of the mist and blocked his path. They were two giants, clothed in animal skins and with the skulls of dead men strung around their waists.

Sir Lancelot was tired and hungry and he was wondering how he could avoid fighting them when he heard someone shouting from the battlements. Looking up he saw that a maiden was trying to attract his attention.

"Ride away while you can, Sir Knight," she cried anxiously. "No one has ever passed these two giants unharmed. They crush the skull of anyone who tries to run away from them."

Lancelot remembered that this was the castle where Arthur was born, and knew he would be unworthy to call himself a Knight of the Round Table if he could not free its inhabitants from their captors. The giants held clubs the size of tree trunks, so he would be no match for them in a straight fight. He would have to outwit them.

Lancelot dismounted and stood in front of the giants. "Good evening, gentlemen," he said craftily. "I hope that you are well? I believe this mist is lifting at last. Would you like to walk with me and admire the view?"

The two giants were puzzled by Lancelot's politeness, for no other knight had spoken to them like this – all the others had ridden away in terror as soon as they saw the fearsome pair.

"We will walk with you, foolish knight, before we kill you," they said agreeably.

Lancelot led them close to the edge of the cliff, and soon the ground began to give way beneath one of the giant's feet. He beckoned to the other giant to come closer.

"Do you want to hear a riddle, my friend?" he said. "Bend down so that I can whisper in your ear."

As the giant did so, Lancelot drew out his sword and with one mighty slash cut his throat and pushed him over the cliff. The remaining giant shook with rage and made the earth tremble beneath him. As he raised his club above his head to strike Sir Lancelot the cliff edge gave way and he also fell down on to the rocks below.

The inhabitants of the castle, who had watched everything happen, streamed out of the castle to greet the knight who had saved them. They knew it could be none other than Lancelot.

When Lancelot rode away from Sir Turquin's castle, Sir Kay had followed after him. He hoped to catch up with the brave knight who had rescued him from the dungeon, and help in his dangerous quests.

One evening as it was growing late, three knights set upon Sir Kay. Although he defended himself bravely, he was no match for them. Far away in the distance Kay could see a light shining, and hoping that it came from a house where he might find refuge, he turned his horse and rode fast towards it, pursued by his three opponents.

Now it happened that the light shone from an inn where Lancelot himself had taken shelter for the night. He had just lain down to rest, when there was a loud knocking at the gate. He looked out of the window and recognized Sir Kay fighting a desperate battle against three other knights. Seizing a sheet from the bed, he threw one end of it out of the window and lowered himself to the ground. Then, sword in hand, he ran to help Sir Kay.

The three strange knights turned on Lancelot, thinking that they would quickly dispose of this man who came against them without any armor, but with a few strokes of his sword Lancelot brought all three to the ground. They begged him to spare their lives, and he told them to go to Arthur's court and give themselves up to the Queen and tell her that Sir Kay had sent them to swear allegiance. The three knights swore that they would do as he asked and then they rode away, very subdued and humbled at having been overcome by a unarmored man.

Lancelot took Sir Kay back to the house and roused the landlord, who let them in and gave them food and wine. As soon as they came into the light, Sir Kay recognized Lancelot, and fell on his knees to thank him for twice saving his life.

Next morning Lancelot rose early while Sir Kay was still sleeping and dressed himself in Kay's armor, leaving his own armor and weapons for Sir Kay. He thought that if Kay wore his armor, everyone would think that he was Lancelot and he would reach home in safety. So, clad in Kay's armor, Lancelot set out once more in search of brave adventures. He was not long in finding them, for he had ridden only a short distance when he saw four of King Arthur's knights resting idly under a tree. They were Sir Gawain and Sir Uwaine, Sir Sagramour and Sir Hector de Maris, Lancelot's cousin. When they caught sight of Lancelot riding towards them in Kay's armor, they thought it was Sir Kay.

"Look who comes here," said Sir Sagramour, stirring lazily. "It's Sir Kay himself. I think I'll challenge him to a duel."

Sagramour took up his spear, mounted his horse and rode towards the approaching knight. The others watched in amusement. They knew that, though Sir Kay was a valiant knight at heart, he was not a very skilful one when it came to deeds of arms.

Lancelot laughed to himself when he saw Sir Sagramour coming to meet him. He guessed that the knight thought he was about to win an easy victory. Setting his spear in rest, he met the onslaught of his opponent, and to Sir Sagramour's astonishment, he knocked him from his horse at the very first blow.

The other knights were amazed, and Sir Hector de Maris took up his spear at once and galloped towards the supposed Sir Kay. But he had no more luck than Sir Sagramour, and at the first blow he found himself stretched on the ground as well.

"It cannot be Sir Kay!" said Uwaine to Sir Gawain. "It must be some strange knight who has overcome Sir Kay and killed him and taken his armor. I will go out and fight him for what he has done to Sir Kay." With that he rode fiercely at Sir Lancelot, not just to joust with him, but with the intention of killing him.

But Lancelot parried his fierce blows as easily as he had been able to parry the friendly strokes of Sir Sagramour and Sir Hector de Maris. And without doing him any serious harm, he gave Uwaine such a blow that he too reeled from his saddle and fell to the ground.

Then Sir Gawain took his shield and spear and rode out determined to avenge his brother knights. But Lancelot disposed of Gawain almost as easily as he had the other three, and then went on his way, smiling at the thought of the four grounded knights that he left behind him.

Sir Gawain and the other picked themselves up ruefully and rode back to King Arthur's court, while Lancelot rode deeper into the forest, to meet with all kinds of dangerous adventures.

Almost a year had passed by the time Lancelot made his way back to Camelot, where Arthur and Guinevere were eagerly awaiting his return. While he had been away his fame had grown greater and greater, for almost every day a knight or lady whom he had helped brought news of his bravery.

Once again all Arthur's knights were gathered together at the Round Table at the Feast of Pentecost, when Sir Lancelot rode into the Great Hall wearing Sir Kay's armor. As soon as they saw him, Gawain and his three companions recognized Lancelot as the stranger knight who had overcome them so easily. They laughed and poked fun at each other over the trick that had been played on them.

Then Sir Kay told the King how Sir Lancelot had rescued him from the three knights who would have slain him. And next all those knights who had been held prisoner by Sir Turquin told how Lancelot had saved them. King Bagdemagus told how Lancelot had fought for him in a tournament and defeated his opponents. Many others came as well and told of Lancelot's gallant deeds, and everyone, high and low, paid honor to him.

So Lancelot's fame spread throughout the land of Britain. King Arthur was happy to have such a brave and gallant knight in his court, and Queen Guinevere loved him well.

TRISTRAM AND ISEULT

ONCE AGAIN, King Arthur's knights had gathered at Camelot to celebrate the Feast of Pentecost. As they took their seats at the Round Table they heard the soft notes of a harp, and a wandering minstrel came into the Great Hall. He was a fine, strong man with noble features, but his clothes were poor and tattered.

"Welcome, good minstrel," said Queen Guinevere. "Come and sing for us. Tell us of noble knights and fair ladies; of chivalrous deeds and brave adventures."

Arthur offered the minstrel some wine. "Where do you come from?" he asked.

"From Cornwall, my lord King," the minstrel replied.

"Then tell us a tale of a Cornish knight."

The minstrel drank the King's health and began his lay, sometimes telling it as a story, and sometimes singing it to the sad, sweet music of the harp.

Just after Mark was made King of Cornwall by Uther Pendragon, King Rivalen of Lyonesse crossed over the sea to help him wage war. Rivalen fought bravely on Mark's behalf and was rewarded with his sister Blanchefleur as a wife. They were married in the great church in Tintagel, but not long after the wedding news came that an old enemy, Duke Morgan, had attacked Lyonesse and was laying waste the countryside all around. Rivalen set sail immediately, taking with him his new wife. Blanchefleur was expecting a child, so he left her in the safety of his castle in Lyonesse and went off to fight.

Blanchefleur waited many months for her husband to come home, but just after her child was born she learned that Rivalen had been slain in battle, and she lost her will to live. She called her infant son Tristram, which means "born in sorrow," and gave him into the care of a faithful follower called Rual before she died.

Rual and his wife looked after Tristram lovingly, and brought him up as if he was their own son. His tutor, Gorvenal, taught him to ride a horse, to use a sword and spear, to sing with the harp and to play at chess. And he took him to foreign lands so that he might learn to speak languages other than his own. By the time he was old enough to become a squire, Tristram was an accomplished youth.

One day a Norwegian merchant ship stopped at Lyonesse to trade, and the captain was entertained at Rual's house. Tristram was invited to go aboard to play chess. While they were engrossed in their game the sailors quietly drew up the anchor, hoisted the sails, and slipped out to sea, taking Tristram with them to sell as a slave. But a storm rose up and tossed the ship about for nine days and nights, until everyone on board feared for their lives. The sailors claimed that a curse had been put on them for stealing Tristram, and so they set him ashore as soon as they sighted land.

It happened that this land was Cornwall. Tristram came to Mark's court at Tintagel and served the King so well that before long he was made a trusted councillor. Then Rual himself, after wandering far and wide searching for the missing youth, came to Cornwall and found Tristram, and said to the King, "King Mark, this is your nephew Tristram of Lyonesse, son of your sister Blanchefleur and of King Rivalen. Duke Morgan holds his land wrongfully, and it is time that land came back to its lord."

Mark was delighted to learn that Tristram was his own nephew. He sent his armies to Lyonesse to kill the usurper and Rual was left in charge. Meanwhile, Mark was having troubles of his own. Some years earlier the Cornish King had been defeated in a war against King Anguish of Ireland, and the tribute owing to the Irish had never been paid. The Irish King was now demanding, in lieu of the dues, thirty boys of noble birth who would be sold into slavery. King Mark sent the messenger away. "Tell your King that if he wants tribute from us then he must send someone to fight for it," he ordered.

When King Anguish received this defiant message he was furious and sent his wife's brother, Sir Marhaus, a fearsome warrior with a shaggy red beard, to settle the matter in single combat. The Cornish King despaired of finding anyone who could stand against Marhaus, and there seemed to be no choice but to send the children as King Anguish demanded.

But then Tristram stepped forward. "Shame on you all!" he cried. "Call yourselves men when you would sell your own sons into slavery! Knight me, and I will be your champion."

King Mark was reluctant to let his nephew risk his life in this way, but as no other champion came forward, he eventually relented. And so it was that Tristram was dubbed a knight and presented with a fine sword and a suit of armor.

The battle was to take place on a little island close to the harbor where the Irish ships were lying. Tristram and his horse were ferried over to the island in a boat, while all the people from the Cornish court gathered on the shore to watch what would happen. When they saw how young their champion was, they were very angry with King Mark for letting so young a knight fight his battle for him. They wept and mourned for the brave boy, thinking that they would never see him alive again.

Sir Marhaus was also shocked when he saw his young opponent, and he did his best to persuade Tristram not to go on with the battle. But Tristram was determined to wipe out the shame his uncle had brought upon the Cornish court, and he insisted that the fight should take place. Marhaus, who was one of the knights of the Round Table, was a chivalrous knight, and he did his best to soften the young man's defeat.

"As you are determined to do battle with me, young knight," he said, "I cannot refuse you. But I make this one condition: if you withstand three of my blows, then you can consider yourself unbeaten, and leave with your honor untarnished."

Then the two knights rode at each other, and with his first stroke Marhaus wounded Tristram in the side. But the young knight would not give in, and although he was in great pain he fought on determinedly. For all his youth, he was as courageous as a more experienced knight. He withstood far more than three of his opponent's blows, and in the end he struck Sir Marhaus on the head with such force that the big man sank to the ground. He was so badly wounded that his men knew he could not recover. They carried him on board ship and sailed back to Ireland, leaving Tristram victor on the island.

Sir Marhaus died very soon after he reached the Irish court. His sister, Queen Isaud, was very upset by her brother's death and as she prepared his body for burial she examined the wound on his head. A piece of Tristram's sword had become embedded in the skull where the blade had splintered. Isaud carefully removed this fragment and put it in a casket. She prayed that one day fate might bring Sir Tristram to Ireland so that she might avenge her brother's death.

Meanwhile Tristram had been taken back to his uncle's court, very ill himself from the blow to his side. No matter what treatment was applied, the wound would not heal, and he grew weaker and weaker, until it seemed as though he too must die. At last King Mark sent for his wise men and they told him that his nephew would never recover so long as he stayed in Cornwall.

"He must go to the country where the spear that wounded him came from," they said. "Otherwise he will never be healed."

Arrangements were made for Tristram to be sent to Ireland. But so that no one would know who he was, he was put into a skiff with only his sword, his shield and his harp, and enough food and water for the voyage. Then the skiff was pushed out to sea so that the currents would carry it across the water. As if they knew the frail craft carried such a vulnerable cargo, the dolphins who lived in those waters guided it on its way.

Iseult the Fair, the daughter of the Irish King, was walking along the shore below her father's castle when she came upon the shipwrecked boat. At first she thought the man inside was dead, but when she looked closer she saw that Tristram was just alive. The sick man was carried up to the castle and Princess Iseult took care of him herself, tending his wound so that it healed properly. Just as the wise men had prophesied, Tristram was soon well again and became stronger each day.

Iseult the Fair was young and beautiful: like many Irish women she had lovely black hair that she wore in a thick plait, and her lips were as red as rubies. Sometimes, when Tristram looked too closely at her, her pale cheeks flushed to match.

Tristram fell deeply in love with Iseult, a love that she was not long in returning. For a short time they were happy together: Tristram taught his young nurse to play the harp, and they spent many hours making music and singing songs to each other. But their happiness did not last long. A Saracen knight, Sir Palomides, came to the court and as soon as he saw Iseult he too fell in love and wished to marry her.

Palomides showered Princess Iseult with gifts, and Tristram was very jealous of this man who could declare his love so openly. Tristram himself did not dare to ask King Anguish for his daughter's hand in marriage, because then he would have to admit who he was and everyone would then know that it was he who had killed Sir Marhaus, who was still mourned by everyone at the Irish court.

Soon after Sir Palomides came to court King Anguish held a tournament in his honor and all the knights came to joust at it. Palomides beat everyone who came against him, until Tristram took up his sword and defeated the Saracen knight. Iseult loved her young knight more than ever after he had fought so bravely for her, but she was not to have much more happiness with him. Her mother, Queen Isaud, saw Tristram's sword lying in his chamber where he left it after the fight and noticed that a small piece was broken from the blade. At once she remembered the piece of steel that she had taken from her dead brother's skull, and she hurried to her own room to find the casket in which she had placed it. When she put this fragment against the gap in Tristram's sword it fitted exactly.

The Queen's was furious when she realized who Tristram was. Snatching up the sword in her hand she rushed in search of the young knight, and would have killed him on the spot if one of the attendants had not managed to restrain her. But now Tristram could no longer stay in the castle where he had been so happy. King Anguish sent for him and told him that he must leave Ireland at once.

"I do not blame you for defending your country," he said. "You only did what a brave knight should. But you cannot stay in my castle any longer."

Iseult wept bitterly when he said goodbye, and promised that she would always be true to him. And Tristram vowed that he would be faithful to her, and would fight for no other lady for the rest of his life.

The Cornish court welcomed Tristram as if he had come back from the dead, for no one knew for certain where his voyage had taken him. There were many feasts and celebrations, and King Mark became jealous that the people held his nephew in such high regard.

Tristram, despite the honor that was paid him, was very sad and lonely. He was always thinking about Iseult, and talked about her all the time, saying how good and sweet and beautiful she was. King Mark had been wondering how he might make peace with Ireland, and when he heard Tristram's description of Iseult he was determined to have her for his wife. King Anguish had no other children, so Mark's marriage to Iseult would produce an heir to both their kingdoms.

Mark sent for his nephew and told him that he wanted to marry Princess Iseult, and that Tristram was to go as an ambassador to Ireland to ask for her hand. Tristram was horrified when he heard his uncle's plan. But King Mark's word was law in his own land, and Tristram was obliged to obey him. He had no choice but to take the ship and the men his uncle provided, and set sail again for Ireland.

This time he did not have such a comfortable voyage. Soon after he set out a fierce storm blew up and the boat was driven away from the Irish coast and carried back to England. It came to land close to Camelot, where King Arthur was holding his court, and Tristram decided to anchor there and set up a pavilion on the shore until the storm blew itself out.

While he was waiting for the waves to grow calm, he heard that King Anguish was at Camelot, having been summoned there by Arthur to account for the death of one of Arthur's knights who had been killed in Ireland. Sir Blamore, a cousin of the knight who had been killed in Ireland, had accused the Irish King of treason, and King Anguish had been ordered to do battle against Sir Blamore, or else to find some other knight to fight for him, to prove that it was by accident and not by design that the Knight of the Round Table had met with his death.

When Tristram heard this news he hurried to King Anguish and begged him, for the love that he bore his daughter, to allow him to take the quarrel upon himself. King Anguish was overjoyed when he heard the young knight's chivalrous offer. He himself was growing old, and Sir Blamore was young and strong and a very powerful knight: there seemed little chance that the King would be able to prove his innocence. He willingly appointed Tristram to fight for him, and a message was sent to Sir Blamore telling him that a champion had been found who would do battle against him on behalf of Ireland.

When the Knights of the Round Table heard that a strange young knight was to fight in place of King Anguish they crowded to the field of battle. They were all eager to see how he would stand up to the powerful Sir Blamore. They were not long in finding out. Tristram quickly overcame him, and then stood over the fallen knight and ordered him to yield and declare that King Anguish was innocent of the crime he was accused of.

But although Sir Blamore had been beaten, he was as brave as Tristram himself. He had no fear of death, and he refused to yield and save his life.

"I have sworn to fight to the death," he said, "and I will not go back on my word or give in to you."

Now Tristram was not sure what to do. He could not bring himself to kill the other knight in cold blood, and yet the terms of the battle required him to do so, if Sir Blamore would not yield and admit the King of Ireland's innocence. But Sir Blamore remained adamant, so Tristram left the field and walked to the dais where the judges sat watching the fight, waiting to declare Tristram the victor.

He knelt down before the judges and asked them to intervene. "It is a shame that this noble knight should be killed," he said, "and yet the rules of war demand that I slay him since he will not yield and save himself. I beg you to put aside this ruling and allow me to let Sir Blamore live."

The judges called all the knights who were watching the fight together and consulted with them as to what they should do. In the end they granted Tristram's request, and Sir Blamore was given his life, even though he would not yield, while the King of Ireland was declared innocent of the murder and allowed to return to his own country. So King Anguish sailed back to Ireland, taking Tristram with him.

Now at that time a dragon was terrorizing the countryside around the Irish court, and King Anguish had promised that he would give his daughter Iseult in marriage to whoever slew the fearsome monster. When Tristram heard this news he went on shore fully armed and sought out the dragon's lair high up among the burnt rocks above a fire-scorched valley. The dragon was asleep, with the half-eaten body of a knight clutched in its great shining claws, but it woke at the sound of the horse's hooves and heaved its great body off the ground.

Tristram held his lance steady and, with his shield in front to protect him, rode forward and charged. The monster opened its jaws to breathe fire but the lance went into its mouth and pierced its throat. Screaming with pain and rage the dragon reared up on its hindquarters. Tristram drew his sword and with one unswerving thrust plunged it deep into the monster's heart. Scalding hot blood spurted out onto the rocks, and as the dragon rolled over and died such a blast of flame came out of its mouth that Tristram's shield melted and dripped from his arm.

Taking the heart of the dead dragon with him, Tristram presented himself at the Irish court. When Queen Isaud heard how he had saved them all from the monster, she forgave him for the death of her brother. Iseult was overjoyed to see her lover again, but her joy did not last long, for Tristram had to break the news that he had come to ask for her hand in marriage to his uncle.

King Anguish did his best to persuade the young knight to marry Iseult himself. "I must fulfil my promise and give my daughter's hand in marriage. I wish that you were to marry her yourself, for I know no man in all the world to whom I would more gladly give her. But if you must keep your word to your uncle, take her to be his wife."

Tristram stood firm in his loyalty to his uncle. "Sir," he said, "I would be breaking my vows of knighthood if I did not honor my word."

And so poor Iseult prepared to go with Tristram to Cornwall to be his uncle's wife.

The Queen realized how sad Iseult's life would be if she married someone she did not love. So she made a love potion and gave it to the maid who was to go with Iseult.

"On the day that my daughter and King Mark are married, give them this potion and make sure that both of them drink it from the same cup," she said. "Then Iseult will find love with her husband and forget her unhappiness."

The maid promised to do as she was asked and the love potion was put into a golden flask and stored away in the cabin on board the ship. But one day, when Tristram and Iseult were alone together in the cabin, they found the golden flask and thought that the maid was keeping the wine for herself.

"Let's toast each other with her precious wine," laughed Tristram, and pouring it into a goblet he took a few sips and then held the cup for Iseult to drink. She drank too, and they both agreed that it was the best wine they had ever tasted. Little did they know that they had brought themselves much pain and sorrow, for now there was no power on earth that could change their passionate love for each other.

All too soon the ship landed at Tintagel and Iseult the Fair was married to Mark, the King of Cornwall. But at night, while the King slept, Iseult would creep out to meet Tristram outside the castle walls – until one day someone betrayed them. The King wanted to have Tristram put to death, but his knights persuaded him to banish the young knight and he was sent away from Cornwall. And now he wanders through the land as a minstrel, singing the song of his love.

At this point the minstrel finished his lay, and there was silence in the Great Hall at Camelot. Sir Lancelot bowed his head in his hands, and tears ran down between his fingers as he thought of his own hopeless love for Guinevere.

"Minstrel," said King Arthur presently, "tell me, how do you know so much about this Sir Tristram of Lyonesse?"

The minstrel smiled sadly. "Because I am he," he said.

A murmur went round the hall when the knights heard this, and King Arthur rose from his seat and stepped down to greet him. "Welcome to Camelot, Sir Tristram," he cried. "There is a place for you at the Round Table – see how your name already appears in gold letters on your seat."

So Tristram became a Knight of the Round Table and rode out to fight for King Arthur, to do great deeds and to rescue ladies in distress.

Many years went by and eventually Tristram married a lady from Brittany who was also called Iseult. She was known as Iseult of the White Hands. Tristram was a kind and considerate husband, but could not love her because his heart was still with his first love, the Queen of Cornwall. Then one day he was wounded with a poisoned spear and the wound festered and would not heal. Tristram thought longingly of Iseult the Fair, and of how she had nursed him when he had been wounded before.

Tristram called his squire and said to him, "Iseult of Cornwall is the only one who can treat my wound. Please set sail to Tintagel and ask her to come to Brittany and cure me. I will be watching for your return. Hoist a white sail on the ship if you bring her with you, and a black one if she will not come."

Iseult the Fair came as quickly as she could, and the squire hoisted the white sail. But by this time Tristram was so weak that he could not rise from his bed, so he asked his wife to look out of the window.

Iseult of the White Hands looked out over the sea and saw the ship with its white sail flying, but she was jealous of the Cornish Queen and so she said to Tristram, "I see the ship ploughing through the waves, and all the sails are black."

Then Tristram turned his face to the wall. "God keep you my love, Iseult the Fair," he murmured. "I shall not see your lovely face again." And with that he died.

When Iseult the Fair found that Tristram was already dead her heart broke and she died soon after.

Tristram and Iseult the Fair were buried in one grave, and over the grave were planted two rose trees, one red and the other white. The two trees leaned towards each other and entwined their branches, and grew into one tree with red and white roses. Never in all the world have there been such faithful lovers as Iseult the Fair and Sir Tristram of Lyonesse.

SIR GARETH,
KNIGHT OF THE KITCHEN

EVERY YEAR at Pentecost, on the anniversary of the day when Arthur was crowned King, all the Knights of the Round Table gathered at Camelot for a feast. It was the custom on these occasions that the King did not sit down to eat until he had heard a tale about a brave adventure or chivalrous deed, or been brought news of a quest, or seen some great marvel.

One year, on the day of the feast, no tales of brave adventure had been brought to the King. It began to look as though it would be a fast day, not a feast day, for the court. Then just before noon, Sir Gawain, who was keeping watch at a window, saw three men approaching on horseback, accompanied by a dwarf. One of the men was taller than the others by at least a foot.

Gawain hurried to the King and said, "Sir, you can sit down to eat now, for here comes someone who looks as though he is bringing us interesting news."

Even as he spoke the tall young man, having dismissed his three companions, came into the Great Hall. He was very young, hardly more than a boy, but he was broad and strong as well as tall. The knights eyed him with approval as he went straight to Arthur's seat on the high dais and greeted him politely. "May God bless you, my lord King, and all the Knights of the Round Table."

"God bless you too, my son," Arthur replied kindly. "Why have you come to my court today?"

"I want you to grant me three wishes, sir. I will ask for my first wish today, and the other two twelve months from now, when you hold your feast again."

"Ask what you will and you shall have it," said Arthur, for he liked this tall young man with his fair hair and honest face, and trusted him on sight.

"My first wish is for food and lodgings for twelve months here at court."

All the knights and ladies stared at the stranger in surprise when they heard his request. They had expected such a noble-looking youth to ask for something better than that from the King. And Arthur frowned a little as he replied, "Surely you want something more than this? You look as though you come from a good family – ask me for a more knightly favor."

"It is all I want – and food and lodgings for my companions, too."

"Why, he's just a beggar!" said Arthur's step-brother, Sir Kay. As High Steward he attended to all the household affairs, and was responsible for the kitchens. Kay knew that it would be his task to feed these vagabonds, and this irritated him greatly. He had enough to do without this additional burden.

But Sir Gawain had taken a liking to the boy and sprang to his defense. "I would swear that he is not a beggar," he cried. "Ask him who he is!"

Arthur motioned to the two knights to keep quiet. "I have never refused hospitality to any man who came to me," he said evenly. "You are welcome to have food and lodging at my court. But tell me, what is your name?"

"That, sir, I would rather not tell you until the time is right."

The King liked brave men who did knightly deeds and was disappointed that such a fine, proud youth should want nothing but food. However, he always kept his word, and having promised to grant the wish, whatever it might be, he would not refuse to grant it now.

He beckoned Sir Kay to his side. "I put this youth into your charge," he said. "Give him whatever he wants to eat and drink – and treat him well, because I am sure he will prove to be the son of a duke or lord."

"He's neither of those," said Sir Kay scornfully. "If he was a gentleman's son he would have asked you for a horse and armor. He must be low-born, or he would not have asked for such low things. I will find him a place in the kitchens and give him as much food as he can eat. By the end of twelve months he will be as fat as a pig!"

The youth went off with Sir Kay to the kitchens and the King and his court sat down to eat. "For although," said the King, "we have heard of no brave deeds or adventures today, we have seen a marvel – a young man who might have asked for honor and glory has asked for only food and lodging!"

So, for a whole year, the young man worked in the kitchens, and Sir Kay never missed an opportunity of taunting and mocking him for his strange request. As he still would not say who he was, he was called Beaumains, or Fair Hands, because his hands were white and soft. Kay gave Beaumains all the rough and dirty jobs to do, but he never complained and was always polite and patient. As soon as his work was done, Beaumains would sneak out to watch the knights jousting and practising their skill at arms. Sometimes he would practise secretly himself and, although he was only a kitchen boy and could not of course take part in any of the contests, he could soon throw a spear further than any other man.

Time passed by and the Feast of Pentecost came round again. As on previous occasions, the King refused to sit down to eat until he heard some strange adventure. But this year he did not have to wait long, because a young girl came into the Great Hall and begged for help.

"I am Lady Linnet, sister of the Lady Lyonesse. My sister is held captive in a castle by a cruel tyrant known as the Red Knight of the Red Lawns. Many knights have tried to rescue her, but none has succeeded. I know that your knights are the bravest in the world, and I have come to ask you to send a champion to fight for her."

"Sir," cried Beaumains, rushing forward, "let this be my quest. Grant my second wish by allowing me to go with this girl to fight for her sister."

Arthur looked at him in surprise. Could this be the same youth who had asked for nothing but food and lodging? Perhaps his earlier feelings about the boy had been right – he was probably the son of some great lord who, for reasons of his own, had chosen this strange way of gaining his first insight into knighthood. He smiled at the

eager young man who stood before him. "Your second wish is granted," he said. "And what is your third wish?"

"To be made a knight by Sir Lancelot. Let him ride with me so that I can prove I am worthy of this honor."

Before Arthur had time to reply the girl stamped her foot angrily on the ground. "Shame on you, King Arthur! Surely you are not going to send a kitchen boy to save my sister?" She rushed from the Great Hall in a fury, mounted her horse and rode furiously away from the court.

The knights and ladies in the hall were too astonished at the girl leaving so abruptly to stop her, and before they could reach the door to see which way she went, something happened to take their minds off her for the time being. A servant came running into the hall crying out that a dwarf was waiting outside the castle with a horse and armor for a knight.

"He is waiting for me," said Beaumains quietly, and he walked towards the door. The whole court, who could hardly contain their curiosity, hurried after him. The dwarf helped him to put on the armor, although there was no shield or spear, and then Beaumains turned to Lancelot. "I am going to ride after the young lady," he said. "It is not right that she should leave this court unaccompanied."

The knights and ladies watched Beaumains as he rode off. In the magnificent armor he looked every inch a knight. Sir Kay, angry that the youth was leaving without his permission, elbowed his way through the crowd. "That kitchen boy might look like a fine knight," he said scornfully, "but I'll soon bring him to his senses."

"Leave the boy alone!" cried Lancelot and Gawain together.

But Kay would not listen to them. He called for his horse and rode after Beaumains; and Lancelot, curious to see what would happen, followed behind.

Beaumains had just caught up with Linnet when Sir Kay overtook him. "Beaumains! Stop! Stop I say!" he shouted. "Don't you know who I am?"

Beaumains turned his horse around when he heard the angry shout. "Of course I know who you are. You are Sir Kay, the rudest and most ungentlemanly knight of King Arthur's court."

This made Sir Kay so furious that he set his spear in its rest and charged. Beaumains had no spear or shield, only his sword with which to meet this fierce attack. But he waited for the right moment and skilfully thrust Sir Kay's spear aside. Then he struck him such a blow that Kay fell from his saddle on to the ground, where he lay in an undignified heap. Beaumains dismounted then, and having satisfied himself that Kay was not dead, and would soon recover, he took his spear and shield and armed himself with them. Sir Lancelot, who had followed close behind, flung Sir Kay across his horse and turned it loose to carry him back to Camelot.

Beaumains hurried after Linnet. She turned when she heard the sound of galloping hooves, and she was still very angry. "Go away, kitchen boy," she said rudely. "You smell of grease and boiled cabbage. Surely you don't think that I will allow someone like you to do battle for me?"

"Say what you like," replied Beaumains calmly, "but I will not turn back. I have promised King Arthur to achieve your quest – and achieve it I will, unless I die in the attempt."

Just then they came to a great black hawthorn tree beside a dark glade. A black banner and a black shield hung from the tree, and beneath it sat a knight wearing black armor. "I should run away now if I were you," said Linnet, "because this is the Black Knight of the Black Lawns."

The Black Knight rose to his feet as they approached: he recognized Linnet. "Have you brought this knight to be your champion?" he asked.

"I certainly have not! This is a kitchen boy from King Arthur's castle who persists in following me. I would be grateful if you would get rid of him."

"Well then," said the Black Knight, taking up his black shield and his black spear, "I'll knock him off his horse and he can walk back to Camelot. It is not seemly for a kitchen boy to ride with a high-born lady."

Beaumains drew himself up proudly. "I am a gentleman of noble ancestry and I will prove it to you," he said. Placing his spear in its rest, he charged towards the Black Knight, who hastily sprang onto his horse and prepared to defend himself. Beaumain's attack was so fierce that his spear pierced the Black Knight's armor and went through his body.

Although he was badly wounded the Black Knight would not give in to his young opponent. He drew his sword and rode at Beaumains again, dealing him several hurtful blows. But then he was thrown completely off balance and fell backwards on to the hard ground with a crunch of metal.

"Shame on you!" cried Linnet. She was mortified at what had happened. "You slew him unfairly." And with that she rode off into the forest.

Sir Lancelot, who had been watching from behind some trees, came forward and saw that the Black Knight was dead. "Young sir, you fought bravely and have proved yourself worthy to be a knight. But first, you must tell me your name. I promise that I will keep it a secret – but I cannot give the order of knighthood to an unknown knight."

"Sir, I am Gareth of Orkney, the youngest son of King Lot and Queen Margawse. Sir Gawain and Sir Agravain and Sir Gaheris are my brothers, but they did not recognize me because they left my father's court when I was still a small boy. I came to Camelot in disguise because I wanted to win my spurs on my own merits rather than because of family ties. That is why I asked my uncle Arthur for food and lodging for twelve months – though I hardly thought I would have to serve him as a kitchen boy."

"It gives me great pleasure to dub you," said Lancelot, drawing his sword from its sheath. "All along I thought you were of noble blood. Kneel, Gareth of Orkney, so that I may make you a knight."

Gareth knelt, and Sir Lancelot touched him on the shoulder with the blade of his sword. "Rise up, Sir Gareth!"

And so Gareth was no longer a humble kitchen boy, but a knight of King Arthur's court. Taking the Black Knight's shield and spear, he rode hurriedly after Lady Linnet.

"Not you again, kitchen boy," she sneered. "Don't you know when you are not wanted?"

Just then a knight mounted on a fine white horse came bursting through the trees. He was dressed in green armor and there were green trappings on his horse's back.

"Greetings, brother," he called in a cheerful voice.

"It is not your brother," said Linnet before Gareth had a chance to reply. "He is King Arthur's kitchen boy."

"Then what is he doing with the Black Knight's weapons?" asked the Green Knight menacingly.

"I won them in fair combat," said Gareth.

"Liar! My brother is a powerful knight and would never be defeated unless he was tricked. Prepare to defend yourself!"

The Green Knight took up his green shield and his green spear and rode at Gareth. The two knights jousted fiercely until their spears were broken into pieces. Then they

fought with swords – on horseback and then on foot.
The Green Knight struck such a hard blow that he cut
Gareth's shield in half; but the brave knight took his
sword in both hands and brought it down on the Green
Knight's helmet. He fell to the ground and lay there
begging for mercy.

Gareth stood over his fallen opponent. "I will spare
your life if this lady begs it from me."

"Me? Beg for his life from you?" cried Linnet.
"That I will never do!"

"Then he must die," said Gareth. He raised his
sword as though he was about to settle the matter by
slaying the Green Knight.

"Wait!" Linnet, even though she had a hot temper
and a fierce tongue, was still a woman. She could not
bear to see a man killed before her eyes. "Do not kill him."

Gareth appeared not to notice her ungracious manner.
He put his sword back into its sheath. "Madam," he said,
bowing low, "your command is my pleasure."

Then turning to the Green Knight he said, "I spare
you at this lady's request, on condition that you go
and swear allegiance to King Arthur and tell him that
the Knight of the Kitchen sent you."

By now it was growing late, so the Green Knight
took Gareth and Linnet to his castle. Linnet was angrier
than ever at Gareth's success and refused to sit with him
at the same table. "I will not eat with a kitchen boy,"
she said haughtily. "He should be eating with the pigs,
not with a high-born lady."

The Green Knight was ashamed at her words.
Whoever Gareth might be, he had proved
himself a knight of honor
and courage.

He led Gareth to a side-table and then sat down there with him, leaving the high-born lady to eat her meal alone. And there she sat in angry solitude, while Gareth and the Green Knight talked and laughed together.

The next morning, as they rode on their way once more, Gareth rebuked Linnet for her rudeness. "I have had enough of your insults," he said firmly. "I have served you honorably and overcome knights who, you said, would beat me. Either you treat me more civilly or I give up this quest."

Just then they came within sight of the walls of the castle where Lady Lyonesse was held captive. As they drew near they saw the dead bodies of many knights hanging from the branches of a Judas tree.

"These are all the knights who came to rescue my sister," said Linnet sadly. "The Red Knight of the Red Lawns overcame them one by one, and put them to this shameful death without mercy or pity. He is the most dangerous knight in the world because he has the strength of seven men. He has laid siege to that castle for many months, and could easily have taken it – but he is in league with Morgan le Fay. They hoped that Sir Lancelot or Sir Gawain would come on this quest, or King Arthur himself, and that the Red Knight would slay him, as I fear that he will slay you."

"I will never give in to this cruel knight!" Gareth reached for the great ivory horn that hung from a branch of the tree and raised it to his lips.

"Wait!" cried Linnet. "Don't blow the horn yet. It is still early in the morning and it is said that the Red Knight's strength grows until the middle of the day, and then wanes in the afternoon until by sunset he is no stronger than other men." She looked up at Gareth from beneath her eyelashes and smiled at him timidly.

Seeing how Linnet had softened towards him strengthened Gareth's resolve to be victorious. "I would be unworthy," he said defiantly, "if I waited to fight with him when his strength has gone."

With that he blew such a blast on the horn that the walls of the castle echoed with the sound of it, and everyone looked out to see who dared to blow it so loudly. Lady Lyonesse herself came to the window, and when she saw her sister with Gareth she knew that yet another brave knight had come to fight for her. She did not know whether to be glad or sorry: so many brave knights had lost their lives for her that she had little hope that this one would succeed.

And then the Red Knight himself appeared, dressed in blood-red armor. With his great red spear in one hand and his red shield in the other, he galloped out to meet the foolhardy knight who dared to challenge him. The two knights came together with a noise like thunder. On horseback and then on foot they fought fiercely until noon, when they were obliged to rest a while, for both of them were exhausted. But soon they were on their feet again and continued fighting until the evening.

At one point Gareth was nearly overcome: he was faint and weak from loss of blood, and in an unguarded moment the Red Knight struck his sword out of his hand. Before he could recover it, he received a stunning blow to his head that knocked him to the ground. But just as the Red Knight was about to deliver the final thrust, Linnet cried out, "Save yourself, my valiant knight! Where has your courage gone?"

When Gareth heard her words and saw the tears streaming down her face he pulled himself together and with a final effort sprang to his feet, picked up his sword and flung himself on the Red Knight. His attack was so fierce and unexpected that the Red Knight staggered and sank at last to the ground.

Then Gareth pulled off the Red Knight's helmet and would have killed him, but he cried out, "Noble knight, I beg for mercy!"

Gareth thought of the dead bodies hanging from the Judas tree. "How can you beg for mercy when you have shown none to all those brave knights?"

"Once I loved a lady even more than my own life. She was lady-in-waiting to Morgan le Fay. Her brother was killed by a knight from King Arthur's court and she made me vow that if I met and overcame any of Arthur's knights, I would show them no mercy but put them to a shameful end."

"You did wrong to make such a vow," said Gareth. "But since it was at a lady's request, and you were influenced by Morgan le Fay, I blame you less. Go to the lady whom you have held prisoner for so long and make amends. If she forgives you, I will forgive you too, and you will go to Arthur's court with all your knights and swear allegiance."

So ended Gareth's quest. When he returned to Arthur's court it was not to take his old place in the kitchen, but to be included among the bravest of the Knights of the Round Table, for now everyone knew his story. And before many weeks had passed he married Linnet, and they lived happily together for many years.

Lancelot and Elaine

From the very first day he came to court Lancelot had loved Queen Guinevere. Arthur was a great king, kind and just, but he was not a great lover as Lancelot was. To Arthur, the excitement of the chase and the honor and glory of battle were more important than his love for his wife. So it is not surprising that in time Guinevere grew to love Sir Lancelot – who served her with such devotion and performed such brave deeds for her sake – better than she loved the King who was her husband.

Lancelot and Guinevere spent more and more time together, often meeting in secret in the Queen's private garden, where no one could see them. And so the first shadow of evil crept into Camelot and set a trap for Sir Lancelot....

One spring day a hermit came to Camelot and greeted those who sat at meat in the Great Hall. "May God bless all who are gathered here," he said, looking around at the assembled company. Then he pointed to the empty seat between Sir Lancelot and Sir Percival. "I see there is one place that remains empty."

"That is the Siege Perilous," Arthur explained. "It is intended for the most noble knight of all, and anyone else who sits there will die."

"The knight who will sit there will be born this year," said the hermit, "and he will achieve the Quest of the Holy Grail.... But I came here today to speak about another quest. There is a lady who has for years been held captive in the Dolorous Tower. Only the best knight amongst you can win her freedom, and that is Sir Lancelot of the Lake. Therefore I beg him to come with me as quickly as possible."

Lancelot left early next morning and rode with the hermit until they came to the city of Corbenic. All the people ran out to welcome him, and as he rode through the narrow streets they threw garlands of flowers around his neck and rose petals under the feet of his horse.

"Welcome, Sir Lancelot," they cried. "A wicked queen has imprisoned our lady in the tower because she is jealous of her beauty. She is kept in a bath of boiling hot water, and can be freed only by the best knight in the world."

Sir Lancelot knew at once that this was the work of Morgan le Fay. "Lead me to her," he ordered.

The townspeople led him to a great black tower, and as soon as he put his hand on the door the bolts and bars broke into pieces. Once inside, the air was unbearably hot and thick steam shrouded the stairway. Finding it almost impossible to catch his breath, Lancelot climbed slowly up the slippery stone steps to a chamber right at the top. The most beautiful lady he had ever seen lay in the bath; her delicate skin was red and wrinkled from the intense heat. Plunging his arms into the scalding water the best

111

knight in the world lifted the lady out of the bath and carried her downstairs.

When the lady had been clothed again by her waiting ladies, she came to Lancelot and said, "I am Elaine, the daughter of King Pelles of the Waste Land Kingdom. Please come with me to my father's castle so that he may thank you for rescuing me."

Lancelot followed Elaine through the desolate landscape of the Waste Land Kingdom to the nearby castle that was her home. King Pelles was known as the Maimed King, because his arm was withered from a wound inflicted by Sir Balin many years before. Pelles could hardly contain his excitement when he heard the name of his daughter's rescuer, for he knew that a prophecy was about to be fulfilled.

That evening, when they sat down to supper in the hall, there was no food or wine on the table. Then suddenly the door burst open and into the hall came three veiled women, dressed in white. The first one carried a spear that dripped blood onto the floor; the second held a golden platter covered with a cloth; and the third a golden chalice. The chalice radiated a light so pure and bright that no one could look at it, and the King and his companions fell to their knees in prayer as it passed. When the women had gone a feeling of peace and well-being seemed to fill the hall, and it seemed to Lancelot that he had eaten and drunk of more than mortal food.

"My lord," he said in a hushed voice, "what does all this mean?"

"Sir," answered King Pelles, "you have seen the cup and platter from which Our Lord Jesus Christ ate and drank at the Last Supper. His body was pierced with that Bleeding Spear as he hung upon the Cross. And in that same cup, which is called the Holy Grail, his blood was caught by Joseph of Arimathea as it ran from the wound. I am a descendant of Joseph of Arimathea and the guardian of these precious relics."

While Lancelot was marvelling at what he had just seen, King Pelles watched him intently. He kept thinking about the prophecy that Lancelot would father a child with his daughter Elaine – a son who would achieve the Quest of the Holy Grail and heal Pelles of his wound. He pondered how this might be brought about, for everyone knew that Lancelot loved and served Queen Guinevere and would never look at another woman.

Elaine had a lady-in-waiting, Brisene, who was an enchantress. With her help King Pelles devised a cunning plan. A man came to Lancelot with a ring, which seemed to him to be the one that Guinevere always wore, and told him that the Queen was waiting for him at a nearby castle. Lancelot was so eager to see her again that without stopping to think he mounted his horse and rode to Castle Case, where he found his beloved Guinevere waiting for him. Finding her alone like this, with her eyes full of love, Lancelot forgot his honor and loyalty to King Arthur and spent the night entwined in Queen Guinevere's arms.

When the bright light of morning streamed into the bedchamber Lancelot found Elaine, not Guinevere, sleeping at his side. Brisene had used her magic skills to change her lady's shape into that of the Queen. When Lancelot realized how he had been tricked he drew his sword and threatened to kill Elaine. But she knelt at his feet begging for forgiveness, and told him about the prophecy that had led to the deception.

Lancelot spared the frightened lady, but he rushed out of the castle like a madman, dressed only in his shirt. He ran deep into the forest until he was completely lost; and there he wandered, cold, hungry and aimless, for many weeks. He managed to survive by eating berries and wild fruit, and drinking water from the streams. Soon he became thin and haggard, and his troubled mind was haunted by visions of strange creatures. In time he became so confused that he did not even know his own name, and could remember nothing about his past life.

When Lancelot eventually found his way back to Corbenic no one realized who he was. The dogs chased him and the young men of the town pelted him with stones. At King Pelles' castle the servants took pity on the half-naked madman: they gave him straw to lie on by the gate, and from a safe distance threw him scraps of meat.

Meanwhile Elaine grew large with child, and nine months after that enchanted night she gave birth to a boy who was christened Galahad. She was walking in the castle grounds one day when she came upon the sleeping madman and recognized him as Sir Lancelot, the father of her child. Elaine's heart filled with compassion when

she saw the emaciated body and haunted face of the once-powerful knight. Taking care not to wake him, she had him carried into the room where the Holy Grail was kept. And in this holy place Lancelot woke to find his memory restored and his madness gone.

With Elaine's tender care Lancelot grew well and strong again, but he was desperately ashamed of what had happened, and his only thought was to hide himself away where no one would find him. So he and Elaine went away to the Joyous Isle, where it was summer all year long, and lived in peace with their little son. But nothing Elaine could do would remove the sadness from Sir Lancelot's eyes, especially when he stood on the shore and turned his gaze towards Camelot.

One day, not far away from the Joyous Isle, a tournament was held, and news of it was brought to Lancelot. When he heard about it, all his old love of adventure and brave deeds came back to him, and he sent a messenger to the tournament to proclaim that he was ready to joust with any knight who wanted to come to his castle and challenge

him. He also promised that, if any knight could beat him, he might choose the best falcon in his falconry.

Many brave knights came forward to joust with the strange knight of whom no one seemed to have heard before, but none of them succeeded in winning Lancelot's prize. No less than five hundred knights came to do battle, but, one after another, the great knight beat them all.

Then two of the knights from Arthur's court, Sir Hector de Maris and his cousin Sir Lionel, came to the Joyous Isle. Back at Camelot, everyone had been wondering what had become of Sir Lancelot, for no one had seen him since he rode off with the hermit. When he failed to turn up for the Feast of Pentecost, Guinevere had sent his cousins, Sir Hector and Sir Lionel, to look for him. They had searched far and wide throughout the land for many months and had almost given up hope of finding Lancelot. But they were always eager for adventures, and when they heard of the challenge they offered to joust with the unknown knight.

Lancelot was ready to try his skill against anyone who came. Sir Lionel was the first to encounter him, and they fought for a long time, neither gaining any advantage over the other. But in the end Sir Lionel was overthrown, and, surprised at the strength of his opponent, he called out, "I have never met such a brave and accomplished knight before. What is your name?"

"My name is Le Chevalier Mal Fet," replied Lancelot. "What is yours?"

"I am Sir Lionel of the Round Table," said the fallen knight as he rose to his feet.

At this Lancelot flung away his sword and dropped to his knees. "My lord King!" he cried. "What have I done to fight against a knight of the Round Table?" And then he told Sir Lionel who he was.

Lancelot was delighted to see his kinsmen after such a long time. They told him how much Arthur and Guinevere missed him and how everyone still thought of him as the best knight in the world. Lancelot began to yearn for Camelot, and before long he told Elaine of his intention to return.

Elaine wept: she knew that Lancelot would never come back to her once he was with Guinevere. She pined for Lancelot when he was gone and lost the will to live: even the laughter of her beautiful little son did not cheer her. Shutting herself away in

her chamber she refused to eat. Soon her body became pitifully thin and it was not long before she faded away.

Elaine's dying wish was that Lancelot should see her wasted and lifeless body and feel some guilt for being the cause of her death. Brisene dressed her dead mistress in rich robes and jewels and then she was laid in the barge that was to take her on her final journey down the river that flowed to Camelot.

Some days later Sir Kay came hurrying into the Great Hall with news of a great marvel. "My lord," he said breathlessly, "there is a black barge covered in white lilies out there on the river, and in it lies a beautiful lady dressed in rich robes and jewels."

Then Arthur, with Guinevere and many of the knights, went down to the river and found that the barge had come to rest against the bank. The King saw that the dead lady held a letter in her hand, and he took it up and opened it.

Most noble knight, Sir Lancelot, I loved you truly. Now death has taken me I beg you to pray for my soul and to give my body an honorable burial.
  Elaine of Astolat

When Lancelot heard this he covered his face with his hands and wept. "My lord King," he said, "I am very sad that it has come to this, but I swear before God that I was not willingly the cause of her death. It is true that she loved me, and wanted more than anything to be my wife. But love cannot be commanded, and it would be dishonorable to wed someone that one did not love."

Elaine was buried in the cathedral at Camelot and the shadow of her death never quite passed from Sir Lancelot. Though he was still called the best knight in the world, he knew he was no longer worthy of this high name. Meanwhile, Lancelot's young son, Galahad, was growing to manhood in an abbey not far from Camelot.

THE GRAIL QUEST

A S THE years passed by there was peace in Britain and fewer and fewer people came to King Arthur's court to seek redress for the wrongs that had been done to them. The Knights of the Round Table spent most of their time holding tournaments at Camelot. They became more and more skilled at arms, but found less and less opportunity to prove their prowess. The young knights rode all over the country in search of adventure, but the older ones hung about at court, waiting for something to happen.

On the eve of Pentecost, some years after Lancelot had returned to Camelot, a young lady rode into the Great Hall. After she had greeted the King and Queen, she called out to the assembled knights, "Where is Sir Lancelot?"

When he was pointed out to her, she went over to him and said, "Come with me, there is something of great importance that you must do tonight."

Lancelot asked what it was, but the lady would not tell him. "You will know when you have come," she said. Sir Lancelot never refused a lady's request, so he called for his squire and told him to saddle his horse.

Guinevere was not at all pleased that Lancelot was going off again. "What!" she cried. "Surely you are not leaving us now, on the night before Pentecost?"

"Madam," said the lady, "he will be with you again by dinner time tomorrow, I promise you."

So Lancelot rode away through the forest with the young lady, wondering what it was that she wanted him to do. They had not ridden very far when they came to an abbey in a clearing among the trees. The lady dismounted and took Sir Lancelot inside to a guest chamber; and then the abbess and her nuns came to him, bringing with them a fair-haired boy of about sixteen years.

"Sir," said the abbess, "we have been looking after Galahad since he was a young child, and now we ask you to make him a knight."

Lancelot had never seen such a handsome and noble-looking boy before, and yet his manner was modest and his face shone with goodness and purity. "If that is what the young man wants, I will gladly do so," he said.

All that night Galahad kept vigil in the chapel of the abbey, and very early the next morning, when the sun had just risen, Sir Lancelot made him a knight. When the ceremony was over Lancelot wanted to take the youth back with him to Camelot, but Galahad shook his head. "I cannot come with you yet," he said, "but I will come soon."

So Lancelot said goodbye to him and was back in Camelot by dinner time, just as the young lady had promised. The King had just returned from the service at the cathedral and was eager to sit down to the feast. But Sir Kay, his High Steward,

reminded him that this was Pentecost – the day when he never sat down to eat until he had heard of a brave adventure or seen some marvellous sight.

"If you sit down now, you will break the custom that you have kept for all these years," said Sir Kay.

"I had forgotten," said Arthur. "In my joy at having my best knight, Sir Lancelot, back in time for the feast, I forgot the vow that I made."

But the King did not have to wait long for his feast. Almost immediately a squire came into the hall crying, "Come quickly, I have just seen something amazing! There is a huge stone floating in the river, with a sword embedded in it. It has become trapped against some reeds on the bank, and when I got closer to it, I could see some words inscribed on the blade."

The King and all the court hurried down to the river bank. There, just as the squire had said, was a great block of red marble that had come to rest close to the shore. A sword with a richly-jewelled hilt was thrust into it, and inscribed on the blade in gold letters, just as the squire had said, were some words.

"What does it say?" asked Lancelot.

The squire leaned forward and peered more closely. "It says, 'For the best knight in the world.'"

Arthur turned to Lancelot. "It must be for you," he said.

But Lancelot shook his head. He thought of his wrongful love for Queen Guinevere, and how Lady Elaine had died of a broken heart, and knew that he was no longer worthy of that high place. "It is not meant for me," he said sadly.

The King turned then to Gawain, his nephew. "You try and pull it out," he commanded.

Gawain was always willing to try anything. He grasped the hilt firmly and pulled, but the sword would not move. Then several of the other knights tried, but none of them were able to pull it out of the stone.

THE GRAIL QUEST

Eventually everyone was so hungry that they gave up trying and went back to their places at the Round Table. Just as they were about to start eating a hermit came into the hall with a beautiful youth dressed entirely in red armor, and Lancelot saw that it was the boy he had knighted that very morning, Sir Galahad.

"I bring you a new knight," said the old man, whose name was Naciens. "He comes from royal blood, and is a descendant of Joseph of Arimathea. You have already seen a great marvel today, but there will be other adventures in distant lands that will greatly surpass anything you have witnessed so far."

"He is welcome," said King Arthur.

At the Round Table there was one place at which no one had ever sat. When the table was first brought to Arthur's court, Merlin told the King that the seat was intended for the most noble knight of all, and anyone else who dared to sit in it would die. The seat had been covered with a cloth ever since, and it was always known as the Siege Perilous, the dangerous seat.

Now Naciens led the youth to this very seat. He removed the cloth that covered it and there, for everyone to see, were some golden letters, "This is the seat of Galahad."

As the hermit turned to leave, Galahad caught hold of his arm and said, "Take my loving greetings to my grandfather. Tell King Pelles that I will soon return to heal his wound and bring the Waste Land Kingdom back to life."

Lancelot, hearing these words, realized that Galahad must be his own son, whom he had not seen since leaving the Joyous Isle. He gazed at him proudly as Galahad took the seat that had been reserved for the purest knight of all.

When dinner was over the King took Galahad down to the river to see the sword that was embedded in the great marble stone.

"This is my sword," Galahad said quietly. "See, I carry its scabbard. It wounded my grandfather, King Pelles. Naciens told me that I would find it here at Camelot." Then he grasped the hilt and pulled the sword effortlessly out of the stone.

Arthur was amazed that the youth had been able to draw the sword out of the marble stone when so many strong knights had tried and failed. But he remembered that once he had been able to do the same thing, and he knew this meant that Galahad was destined for some great quest.

That night, when the King and his knights were eating their supper at the Round Table, there was a great clap of thunder that shook the walls of the castle and made the doors slam shut. All the knights except Galahad sprang to their feet, thinking that the walls were about to fall on them. Then a brilliant ray of light shone through the Great Hall, brighter by far than the brightness of the midday sun. And down the ray glided a vision – a chalice gleaming beneath a veil – and the knights knew that it was the Holy Grail itself. The light was so dazzling that none of them could have seen the sacred vessel clearly, even if it had not been veiled by the cloth.

The knights stood in silent awe, holding their breath in amazement, until the vision disappeared. When they sat down again, they saw that each man's plate held the food he liked best, put there by unseen hands as the Grail passed through the hall.

Some of the knights felt uneasy about what they had just seen, but Sir Gawain, who was always ready to rush into any adventure, rose to his feet. Without stopping to consider whether he was worthy to undertake such a great quest he said, "We have all been served with the food we like best, but could any of us see the chalice clearly? It was so well covered, I could hardly distinguish its shape. Tomorrow I am going to ride out in quest of the Holy Grail, so that I can see it without the veil."

When the other knights heard Gawain's rash vow, they too swore that they would ride out in quest of the Holy Grail. King Arthur was upset when he heard the vows they made, because he knew that few of them, if any, were worthy to accomplish the Quest. Only a knight who was pure in mind and body would be able to look at the holy cup without its veil. Though they were noble and brave, the Knights of the Round Table could not claim such perfection as this. Now that they had sworn, they must try to fulfil their vows, even if there was little hope of their being able to do so.

"I cannot deny you this adventure," said Arthur sadly. "But I fear that many of you who ride out on this Quest will never return to Camelot again."

Some of the knights began to regret their hasty vows, but it was too late to draw back now. When morning came, the King, and all those who had vowed to ride out on the Quest, went to the cathedral to hear mass before starting on their journey. Then they said goodbye to their weeping ladies and rode out of Camelot.

The new young knight, Sir Galahad, was one of those who rode out on the Quest of the Holy Grail. When he left Camelot he was still without a shield, but he had been told that both sword and shield would be given to him in due course. The sword had already been provided, and he knew that the shield would come to him when the proper time came.

For four days Galahad rode through the forest without meeting with any adventures. On the evening of the fourth day he came to an abbey where two other knights were staying, and he decided to spend the night there with them, as it was growing so late. At this abbey there was a wonderful silver shield with a red cross in the center, which was said to bring death or disaster to any man who carried it, unless he was the best knight in the world. The monks had been guarding the shield carefully until its rightful owner came to claim it. But though many knights had attempted to carry the shield away, all of them had met with death or sustained a terrible wound.

King Bagdemagus was one of the knights staying at the abbey, and he decided that he was going to try and take the shield. "I know that I am not the best knight in the world," he said to Galahad, "but I want to try this adventure. Please remain here for three days, and if I fail in this quest I can think of no worthier knight than you to claim the shield."

The next morning he took the shield down from behind the altar where the monks had hung it and rode away. But Bagdemagus was not allowed to ride far with the shield. He had only gone a short distance when a strange knight dressed in shining white armor came galloping towards him and knocked him out of the saddle.

"Only the best knight in the world may carry this shield," said the White Knight as he stood over his fallen opponent. Then he turned to the squire who was standing to one side. "Take your master back to the abbey and give the shield to Sir Galahad," he commanded.

When the monks heard the squire's story, they took the wounded Bagdemagus into the abbey and blessed the young knight as he set out on his Quest once more, this time armed with both sword and shield.

As Galahad was leaving the abbey the squire hurried after him. "Make me a knight, Sir Galahad," he begged, "and let me ride with you on your Quest. My name is Melias, and my father is the King of Denmark."

So Galahad made Melias a knight, and they set off together. Soon they, too, met the White Knight. But this time he made no attempt to take away the shield. He drew rein when he reached Galahad's side, and saluted the young knight courteously. Galahad returned the salute, and when he had thanked the White Knight for sending him the shield, he asked him where it came from.

"It once belonged to an English king who lived in the days of Joseph of Arimathea," said the White Knight. "At one time it had no cross on in, but when St. Joseph lay dying, the King, who had loved and followed him in many of his wanderings, begged that he would leave him a token by which he might remember him. St. Joseph told him to bring his shield, and the saint traced a cross on it with his own blood. This same shield has been kept for you, Sir Galahad, because it is ordained that you shall achieve the Quest of the Holy Grail."

The White Knight then vanished from sight, and for two days Galahad and Melias trekked through the forest until they came to a place where the track divided. As they were deciding which path to follow, a man appeared and said, "Sirs, you must choose now which side you will take. The one who chooses the right-hand path will have an easy journey. The left-hand path leaves all but the best knight open to attack."

"I'll take the left-hand path!" cried Sir Melias, who was longing to prove himself as a knight. He rode off into the forest before Galahad could stop him.

Before long Melias came to a clearing in the forest, and in the center there was a throne carved from the trunk of a tree and a golden crown on the seat of the throne. He picked it up and put it on his head. As he did this a knight on a powerful warhorse crashed out of the nearby trees.

"Defend yourself!" bellowed the knight as he charged at Melias. "You have taken a crown that is not yours."

Melias set his spear in its rest and rode against him, but he was knocked from his horse and fell wounded to the ground. The strange knight grabbed the crown and rode away, leaving Melias almost dead.

Galahad had taken the right-hand path, which wound through the forest and joined up with the one that Melias had followed. He came into the clearing just in time to see the strange knight riding away. "Turn, coward!" he cried.

The knight wheeled round and rode furiously at Galahad. Their spears cracked together, but Galahad's struck home, piercing the other knight's shoulder and passing straight through his body. With a startled gasp of pain he fell to the ground.

"You fight well," said the strange knight as he staggered to his feet. "I yield to you. Do not worry about your companion. I will look after him and tend his wound, for I am a hermit and skilled in the healing arts. Sir Melias was overcome because he showed pride in choosing the left-hand path, and greed in taking the golden crown."

Then the hermit gave Sir Galahad his blessing and the young knight set off once more on his Quest. This time he rode alone, meeting with many adventures.

Meanwhile, wherever Sir Percival went on his travels, he heard stories of the brave deeds of a knight in red armor who carried a silver shield with a red cross. Then one day he met a hermit who told him that this would be the knight to succeed in the Grail Quest, and that he would surpass his father in strength and glory. Percival realized that this knight was Galahad, and decided to look for him so that he could be his companion in the Quest.

One night, after his horse had been slain in a fight, he fell asleep under an oak tree and woke to find a strange woman standing beside him, her eyes flashing in the moonlight.

"Sir Percival, what are you doing here?" she asked.

"My horse has been killed," he answered, "and I was walking through the forest on foot when I was overcome with tiredness."

"If you promise to help me when I need it, I will bring you a horse."

Percival agreed to this eagerly. The woman went away for a few minutes and then came back leading a magnificent black stallion. Percival took the bridle in his hand and leapt onto its back, and immediately the horse took off into the dark night. Away it went into the forest, on and on through the moonlight. Then in the darkness Percival could hear the sound of a rushing torrent, and it seemed as if the horse was going to carry him right into the middle of a flooding river. He tugged at the bridle, but the horse would not stop. As they reached the dark, foaming water Percival prayed to God and made the sign of the cross, and the horse reared and threw the knight off his back. Then, with a horrible neigh, it plunged into the torrent and was lost from sight.

Sir Percival knelt on the bank and gave thanks for his safekeeping, for he knew that the stallion had been a fiend who tried to carry him to Hell. He remained in prayer for the rest of the night, and in the morning he saw another strange thing.

A huge lion came down to the river to drink, and as it bent over the water a serpent fell from an overhanging rock and twined itself round the lion's neck as if to strangle it. A desperate fight began between the two beasts, and it looked as though the serpent would soon win. The lion roared as if asking for help, so Percival drew his sword and cut off the serpent's head. Then the lion rubbed its head against him, and fawned on him like a cat.

Though the lion was large and fierce, thought Percival, he was still caught unaware by the serpent, and had to call on me to help – just as I would have been killed if I had not prayed to God when I was riding the devil horse.

The lion was now Percival's friend and would not leave his side. They wandered for many days through wild and desolate countryside, and at night Percival slept snuggled against the lion for warmth.

One day Percival sat with the lion on the shore, looking out over the sea, when a ship appeared on the horizon. As it came closer he saw that it had been caught in a storm: the black sails hung in tatters and everything on deck was blackened as if it had been struck by lightning. A lovely young woman dressed in ragged black robes clung to the broken masthead.

"Percival, Percival!" she cried weakly. "Please help me and I will tell you where to find the knight who wears red armour and carries a silver shield with a cross in the centre."

"Madam, I will gladly help you," said Percival. He clambered down over the rocks to the boat and helped the lady safely on to the shore.

"Good Percival, you have saved my life and I will always be in your debt. The knight you are looking for rests at a hermitage nearby, and I will lead you to him."

The lady led Percival along the seashore until they came to a little glade carpeted with grass and flowers, where a silken pavilion was pitched. The day was hot and sultry, and Percival was feeling tired.

"Here, noble sir, you may rest during the heat of the day." Percival took off his armor and lay down on a couch spread with cool silk sheets. He slept for the rest of the day, and when he woke he found the lady waiting for him beside a table set with the finest meal he had ever seen. She offered him wine in a great golden bowl: it was the strongest wine he had ever tasted. And when Percival had drunk she filled the bowl once more, all the time singing a low, mysterious song, and moving closer and closer until her arms were around him.

Percival had never been so close to a woman before, and he began to experience amorous feelings. "Lady," he said in a broken voice, "you are very beautiful."

"Sir," she murmured, "I am yours for ever and ever. I love you more than any man in the world. Kiss me now and swear that you will be mine alone, and do everything that I ask of you."

Percival bent forward to kiss her, but as he did so he caught sight of his sword, which leaned against a tree with the hilt uppermost flashing in the evening light like a

great shining crucifix. In that moment he realized what she had asked of him, and he cried out to God for help, making the sign of the cross on his forehead. Immediately a roaring wind tore the pavilion away, sucking it up into the air where it disintegrated in a cloud of black smoke. Then, with a blood-curdling scream, the lady was transformed into a huge black raven and flew away.

Percival was very upset that he had so easily been deceived by yet another fiend. He knelt down and gave thanks for his deliverance, and then slept beneath a tree until morning. He woke to find a woman dressed in the white robes of a nun, with an ivory crucifix hanging round her neck, bending over him.

"Wake up, Sir Percival," she cried. "Get up and put your armor on. You have overcome the temptations of this world, and now you may go on aboard the Enchanted Ship and sail towards the city of Corbenic. Soon Sir Galahad will be with you on the ship, and Sir Bors too. Do not be afraid – I am your sister Dindrane, though you do not know me, and Naciens, the holy hermit of Corbenic, has been my instructor."

So Percival put on his armour and went down with his sister to the place where the Enchanted Ship was waiting for them.

Many of the knights who had embarked on the Quest for the Holy Grail had grown weary of their adventures and returned to Camelot. But Sir Bors, who was a cousin of Sir Lancelot, continued his journey through many lands until one day he came to a dark forest and saw a tall, lifeless tree. A strange black and white bird that appeared to be half raven and half swan was sitting on a nest right at the top.

That night, while he slept on the forest floor, Sir Bors dreamed about this creature and it seemed to speak to him, offering him all the riches in the world if he would do as it asked. When he woke up the dream was still vivid in his mind, and he wondered what it all meant.

Sir Bors rode on through the forest until he came to a place where the path divided into two overgrown tracks. On one side were two knights leading a horse. A naked man was bound to the saddle and the knights were beating him with hawthorn twigs until blood ran down to the ground. Bors rode up to intervene and saw to his horror that the naked man was his brother, Sir Lionel. He was just about to attack the two knights when he heard a cry from the other track.

"Help me, good sir! Help me!" Turning round, Sir Bors saw a beautiful young girl struggling with an armed knight, who was dragging her towards his horse.

Poor Bors did not know what to do, with both his brother and a young girl in danger. But one of the oaths he had sworn as a knight was that he must not ignore any lady in need of his help. So he prayed to God to keep his brother safe, and then, having made his choice, rode off after the knight who had abducted the maiden.

"Sir Knight!" he cried. "Release the lady at once or I will slay you from behind."

The knight tried to escape by riding more quickly, but as Sir Bors gained on him he let the maiden slip to the ground and turned to fight. Bors was ready to meet the attack and killed him with one thrust of his spear.

"Thank you, noble sir, for saving my life," said the grateful lady. "Please will you accompany me to my home, which is just close by? I am frightened that I may meet other men like him in the dark forest."

"Certainly I will," said Bors gallantly, and he rode with her to a high tower built on a hill.

The young lady made Bors welcome and a lavish feast was prepared in his honor. But Bors had vowed to eat only bread and water until the Quest for the Holy Grail was accomplished, so he would not even taste the fine food that she set before him. Neither would he sleep on the soft bed that had been prepared, but lay down on the hard stone floor among the rushes.

In the middle of the night the young lady came to Bors and tried to tempt him to make love to her, but he refused her advances. This made her really angry, and she led him up to the top of the tower where twelve maidens stood in the moonlight.

"If you will not love me then I will order these ladies to jump from the tower. Do you really wish to be the cause of their death?"

But still Bors would not give in to her. He prayed to God for guidance, and at the very moment that he made the sign of the cross on his forehead the moon disappeared and there was a great rushing of wind. With a fearful screaming like fiends from Hell all the maidens were sucked up into the air and dissolved into streaks of black soot, which fell back to earth in a shower. When the moon came out again Sir Bors found himself alone on the bare hillside, and there was no sign of any tower.

Sir Bors continued on his way and had not ridden far before he met a hermit, who told him that the strange bird he had seen the day before represented the struggle of good against evil. Bors had emerged victorious, but this was little comfort to him because he knew he had done wrong in not saving his brother. He hurried on through the forest, hoping desperately that Sir Lionel was still alive.

Just as he was about to give up hope of finding Sir Lionel, Bors came to an abbey surrounded by beautiful cedar trees and lush green lawns. As he rode up to the gates he saw a knight on the path ahead of him, and drawing closer he saw to his joy that it was his brother. He dismounted and ran towards Lionel with open arms.

"Brother, I thought you had been killed. How glad I am to see you alive and well!"

But Lionel scowled at him and said angrily, "If I am alive, it is no thanks to you! You left me to be tortured and killed by those two knights. Don't come near me unless you want to fight." Then he drew his sword and lunged at Bors.

When Bors realized that he must fight with his brother or die, he did not know what to do. Lionel struck him forcefully on the arm and was just about to slash at his head when a cloud of crackling blue flame came between the two brothers and they were forced to raise their shields to protect themselves from the heat.

Then they heard a voice coming from a little way off, "Brothers, do not kill each other, or you will forfeit your eternal souls." It was Naciens, the hermit of Corbenic, who explained that Lionel had been possessed by a demon who wanted to destroy Bors.

Naciens then told Sir Bors to mount his horse and ride to a ship that he would find at anchor on the shore. When he climbed aboard he found Sir Percival waiting for him, and both knights knew that as soon as Sir Galahad arrived, they could continue on the final adventure of the Grail Quest.

During this time Sir Galahad had been having all kinds of wonderful adventures. Everywhere he went he fought against wicked tyrants, righted wrongs, set prisoners free and helped ladies in distress, so that his name was now famous throughout the land. Not once did he yield to temptation or commit a sin, for he knew that only by remaining pure could he hope to achieve the Quest of the Holy Grail.

One night Galahad took refuge in a hermitage, and while he was resting, there was a loud knocking at the door. The hermit got up to see who was there, and found a young girl standing outside, holding a palfrey by the bridle.

"Sir, I wish to speak to the knight who is staying with you," she said.

The hermit went back, and when Galahad came to the door the girl said, "Arm yourself, Sir Galahad, and come with me. I am Lady Dindrane, Sir Percival's sister, and I have been sent to help you on your great adventure."

Galahad knew that she had been sent to him by God, and he took up his arms and rode after her. Lady Dindrane did not speak until they came to the seashore where the Enchanted Ship was waiting. Then she turned to Galahad and said, "This ship will carry us to the land where you will achieve the Quest of the Holy Grail."

Galahad dismounted from his horse and turned it free, and then followed the girl on board the ship, where to his great joy he found Sir Percival and Sir Bors.

At the start of the Quest, Sir Lancelot had soon parted from the rest of the knights. He had no definite plan in his head, and rode in whatever direction seemed best at the time. His path led him through a great forest, but after a while the trees petered out and he found himself in a dreary waste land. It was just beginning to get dark when he saw a chapel in the distance, and he rode towards it, hoping to find shelter.

When he reached the chapel he found that it was a ruin, but to his surprise there was an altar covered with a white cloth, and on it stood two silver candlesticks with six branches, each with a brightly burning candle. Lancelot tried to enter the chapel, but some invisible force seemed to stand in his way and he could not pass through the open door.

By now it was getting late, so he went back to his horse and unharnessed it so that it might rest. Then he put his shield on the ground and fell asleep upon it.

As Lancelot slept he had a wonderful vision. It seemed to him that two white horses came by, carrying a litter between them. On the litter lay a sick knight, who moaned and cried aloud, "Oh God, when will I be cured of this sickness by the holy vessel that I seek?"

Then invisible hands set up a little table beside the litter and the silver candlesticks floated out of the ruined chapel and came to rest on it. Then the Holy Grail itself appeared on the table, and the sick knight's face lit up with joy when he saw it. He crawled from his litter and knelt before the table, then took the cup in his hands and drank from it. And as he did so his sickness left him and he was perfectly well again.

A squire came, bringing arms and armor, and the two men looked down at Lancelot. In his dream he heard the knight say, "This knight has entered into the Quest of the Holy Grail, but he is not worthy to look upon it, except in his sleep."

The knight took the armor his squire was carrying and dressed himself in it. Then it seemed to Lancelot that the knight took the shield, upon which he himself was lying, from under him and his sword, and mounted Lancelot's horse and rode away.

As Lancelot began to wake up and lay in a half-awake and half-asleep state he heard a voice above him say, "Sir Lancelot, you must go from here, for you are not worthy to stay in this holy place."

Then Lancelot roused himself fully, and found to his consternation that his shield, his sword and his horse had all gone. And he went away from that place on foot, with a heavy heart. "I see now that I should not have undertaken this holy Quest," he said to himself sadly.

Lancelot walked on through the waste land until he reached a little hermitage at the bottom of a hill, where a hermit was saying mass. He stayed until the service was over, and then the hermit, who had seen him weeping, came to him and asked if there was anything he could do.

Lancelot told the old man about the adventure he had undertaken and the vision he had seen the night before, and how he was not worthy to have ridden out on such a holy quest. "All the brave deeds that I have done I did for the love of Queen Guinevere rather than for the glory of God," he sobbed.

When the hermit had heard the whole confession, he placed his hands on Lancelot's bowed head and told him to take comfort. "You are a good man and a brave

knight. God will have mercy on you if you love Him as much as you have loved your Queen. But you will never see the full beauty of His holy cup, because only those who are completely pure can see beyond the veil."

The hermit gave Lancelot a hair shirt and told him to wear it always, and so remind himself to bear arms for God's sake and not only for love of the Queen. And he also gave him a horse, a shield and a sword to replace the ones that he had lost.

So Lancelot rode on his way once more and had many adventures and overcame difficulties that might have daunted lesser men. After some months had passed he came to a castle that was guarded by two lions, and he heard a voice say, "If you have the courage to enter the castle, you will see part of what you desire."

Lancelot hesitated for a moment, wondering whether he should draw his sword to protect himself from the lions. But remembering what the voice had said, he went towards them unarmed, and they drew back to let him through and allowed him to enter the castle unharmed. As he went along he found that every gate and doorway

136

was open, until he came to a room whose door was firmly shut. He could hear singing inside the room – singing that was sweeter than any he had ever heard on earth – and he knew that within the room was the holy cup that he had come so far to see.

Kneeling down, Lancelot prayed to God to grant him just one look at the precious vessel; and as he prayed the door opened and a brilliant light shone on him. Lancelot sprang to his feet and would have entered the room, but a voice said, "No, Sir Lancelot, do not enter the room." So he drew back and bowed his head sadly, disappointed that he was not allowed any closer to the Holy Grail.

After a while he lifted his head again, and inside the chamber he saw an altar surrounded by angels holding candles in their hands. And on the altar was the holy cup itself, covered with a cloth. A priest stood by the altar, and as Lancelot watched, he took the cup, still covered with the cloth, and lifted it up towards heaven. It seemed to Lancelot that the cup changed into the figure of a man – the Savior himself.

The priest staggered a little under the weight of the cup and Lancelot, forgetting the warning he had been given, sprang forward to help him. Immediately a sheet of fire came between Lancelot and the altar, and he was flung backwards on to the ground. Invisible hands lifted him up and carried him out of the room, and then a great darkness fell on him.

For twenty-four days Lancelot lay on the ground outside the room, unable to move or speak. And then on the twenty-fifth day he came out of his trance and gave thanks to God for granting him a glimpse of the Holy Grail. For though he had not seen it unveiled, he had seen more than most mortal men.

So Sir Lancelot rode back to Camelot, and from that time on he wore a rough hair shirt next to his skin in penance for his wrongful love for the Queen. But as soon as he saw Guinevere again, Lancelot knew that he could not stop loving her.

Now the story returns to Dindrane, Sir Galahad, Sir Percival and Sir Bors in the Enchanted Ship, which sailed of its own accord until it came to land beside a castle. As they had no food on board they went ashore to ask the people who lived in the castle to give them some. But as they approached the gates an armed knight rode out.

"You will not leave here until this maiden has yielded to the custom of the castle," he cried. As he spoke many other knights ran out and surrounded the travellers, and several ladies came hurrying after them. One of the ladies held a silver bowl in her hands, and the knight told them that every maiden who came to the castle had to give enough blood from her right arm to fill the bowl.

The three knights were very angry when they heard of this cruel custom, and Galahad cried, "While I am alive you will not touch this maiden!"

Percival and Bors set upon the knight and his attendants and drove them back through the gates. But no sooner had they driven back the first party, than other knights came out to do battle with them. This continued until nightfall, and then the knight who had first accosted them called for a truce and invited them to go into the castle and rest.

"On our honor as knights we will do you no harm," he said. "But tomorrow we must fight again, unless this maiden will yield to the custom of the castle."

So the three knights and Dindrane went into the castle, and they were treated courteously and given everything they wanted to eat and drink. Then Galahad asked why such brave and gallant men should keep such an evil custom.

The knight told them a sad story. "Our mistress has been ill and in terrible pain for many years, and it has been prophesied that she will not get better until she has been anointed with the blood of a maiden who is pure in heart and mind as well as in her body. Many maidens have already given their blood to try and heal our beloved mistress, but still she lies at death's door. We have therefore sworn a vow that no maiden shall pass the castle gates until she has given her blood."

Lady Dindrane listened to this story attentively, and her heart was full of pity for the poor lady who suffered such dreadful pain. She begged her three companions to let her give blood and see if she could save the lady's life. They were very reluctant to allow her to do this. "If you lose so much blood, you may die yourself," said Galahad.

"What does it matter?" Dindrane replied. "If I am found to be as pure in heart and mind as I am in body, the lady may be healed and then this wicked custom will end."

In the end the three knights were obliged to let the brave girl have her way, and when the lady of the castle was anointed with Dindrane's pure blood she was cured of her illness. But she was only healed at the cost of Lady Dindrane's life, for the young

girl became so weak from loss of blood that she fell into a faint and there was nothing anyone could do to save her.

Dindrane smiled up at Sir Percival as she lay dying. "Brother, do not weep for me," she said. "It was ordained that this should be so. As soon as I am dead, lay my body in a boat and let the wind take it out to sea. And when you arrive at the city where you will achieve the Quest of the Holy Grail, you will find me waiting for you. Bury me in that city, and you will one day be buried with me in the same place."

Percival promised to do as she asked, and when she was dead he carried her body to a barge and covered it with a pall of black silk. No sooner had he done this than a wind arose and blew the barge out to sea.

The three knights then returned to the Enchanted Ship, which sailed on until it came to the Waste Land Kingdom. When they went ashore they found horses waiting for them, and they rode inland until they reached Corbenic Castle. As they entered the hall they saw the frail figure of King Pelles, the Maimed King, lying on a wooden bier. He raised himself feebly to see who approached, and was overjoyed when he saw that one of the knights was his grandson, Sir Galahad.

"Welcome, good knights, welcome," he cried. "The end of your quest is near, for tonight the Holy Grail will be in the castle."

He ordered a feast to be prepared and the three knights had just taken their places at the table when a great wind blew through the hall and the doors burst open to admit the procession of the Grail for the last time. Three veiled maidens glided in carrying the Bleeding Spear, the golden platter, and the golden chalice covered with a cloth, and placed them on a silver table at the far end of the hall.

Then a voice called out, "Approach the Grail, Sir Galahad, for you are the purest of all knights. You have no pride or cowardice, or any of the other weaknesses of men."

Sir Galahad went up to the table and lifted the Holy Grail in both hands. Drawing away the cloth, he raised the cup to his lips and drank. Then he took up the Bleeding Spear, and going over to where King Pelles lay on his bier he held it so that the drops of blood fell on to his grandfather's wound. Straight away the wound was healed, and the assembled company dropped to their knees and gave thanks to God for the miracle.

Then once again the voice called out, "Sir Galahad, prepare to leave this land, for tonight you will escort the Holy Grail to its final resting place in the city of Sarras. Take Sir Percival and Sir Bors with you as your companions on the journey."

The three knights set out to ride back to the Enchanted Ship, and as they passed through the Waste Land Kingdom they saw that it had come back to life again, and the air was filled with the scent of flowers that had suddenly bloomed in the night. The ship was waiting for them where they had left it, and when they went below deck they found the Holy Grail covered with a gleaming red cloth, resting on the silver table they had seen at the castle.

For many weeks the ship sailed on its course until at last it arrived at the city of Sarras. As the three knights landed, they saw a barge coming into the shore, and they recognized it as the one in which they had placed the dead Dindrane. "My sister has kept her promise to me," said Percival, weeping.

Then the knights went back to the Enchanted Ship and brought out the silver table and the precious cup covered with the red cloth. The people of the city flocked to see the knights who had brought the Grail. The King of Sarras had recently died, and so they begged Galahad to become their ruler. He built a little chapel in the palace to house the Grail, and every day the knights went there to pray. Percival gave Dindrane's body a royal burial in that chapel.

For a year Galahad ruled the city wisely and well. When the anniversary of his coronation came round, the three knights got up very early in the morning and went into the palace chapel to pray. As they approached the Holy Grail a brilliant beam of light fell upon Galahad, so bright that Percival and Bors had to hide their eyes. And when they could see again, the Grail had gone from its sacred resting place and so had Sir Galahad.

Sir Percival and Sir Bors mourned for the loss of the good knight who had been their companion, and they went to live in a little hermitage outside the city. Percival had not long to live, and died soon afterwards. Sir Bors buried him beside his sister and then set sail for Camelot.

He arrived on the Feast of Pentecost three years after the knights had ridden out. He found Arthur and his court gathered about the Round Table, but now many places were empty, for many knights had died on the Quest. That day there was no need for the King to wait for news of an adventure, for Bors related the whole story of how Sir Galahad had achieved the Quest of the Holy Grail.

MORDRED'S PLOTS

As ARTHUR had feared, the Quest of the Holy Grail proved to be the beginning of the end for the Round Table. Many of the knights who had ridden out on the Quest failed to return, and those who did come back had grown sad and changed, as though they knew that Arthur's glorious reign was drawing to its close.

Sir Lancelot was the most changed of all the knights. He still loved the Queen with passionate devotion, but no longer showed his love for her in the way that he used to. Guinevere was hurt by the change in him: she, too, still loved her knight as much as ever, and she often reproached him for his diminished affection. Eventually Lancelot was unable to endure her reproaches any longer, and spent more and more time away from the court. Only Sir Bors, his cousin, knew where he went.

Arthur remained blind to the love that existed between Guinevere and his favorite knight. The burden of ruling for so many years had taken its toll on him, and he had aged rapidly while his knights were away on the Grail Quest. He and Guinevere had no heir, and now he began to worry about who would succeed him and keep the peace that he had worked so hard to achieve.

Meanwhile Mordred, Arthur's son by his half-sister Morgan le Fay, had grown into a pale and fragile-looking youth with bright red hair. When he reached the age of knighthood his mother sent him to the court at Camelot, revealing his true identity as Arthur's son. The King's rage at his sister's treachery and evil plots had diminished with the passing of years and he had long forgotten Merlin's prophecy that Mordred would one day bring about his destruction. He welcomed Mordred to the fellowship of knights and gave him a seat at the Round Table.

Although Sir Mordred had a weak and sickly appearance, his intellect was very sharp. He had soon discerned the intensity of feeling that existed between Guinevere and Lancelot, and was probably the only person who guessed the real reason behind Lancelot's absences.

Under Morgan le Fay's influence Mordred had become vengeful and evil. He saw himself as the next king of Britain, and wanted to bring this about as soon as possible. Mordred began to sow seeds of resentment against his stepmother, Guinevere. He suggested to some of the knights that she was plotting with Sir Lancelot to usurp the throne and to poison any possible heirs who might stand in their way, such as Sir Gawain, who was nephew to the King. Sir Lancelot, he said, had become arrogant because of the glory his son Galahad had won in the Grail Quest, so he now believed himself worthy to be king. Mordred gained the support of several dissatisfied knights and before long he had gathered around him a loyal band of followers who talked of treason against the King.

With Sir Lancelot away so much, Guinevere became bored and unhappy. Because she was too proud to let people see that she was suffering, she hid her grief in pleasure and organized a sumptuous feast. Twenty-four of the most favored knights were invited to the Queen's private chambers, and Guinevere ordered that special delicacies were prepared for each guest.

Sir Gawain was very fond of fruit, so Guinevere had set a dish of apples on the table especially for him. However, before Gawain had a chance to sample them, another knight, Sir Patrice, helped himself to the choicest-looking apple and as soon as he had taken a bite fell to the floor clutching his throat and gasping for air. Moments later he was dead.

All the knights got to their feet and started shouting accusations. "The Queen has poisoned the fruit!"

"She wished me dead," cried Sir Gawain angrily.

"She is guilty of murder," said Sir Mador, who was a cousin of the dead knight.

Guinevere protested that she was innocent, but nobody believed her. The King and the rest of the knights were sent for, and they gathered in the Great Hall to decide how justice should be done.

"The Queen must stand trial," said Mordred firmly. And those knights that he had won over to his side murmured in agreement.

Arthur was dismayed by what was happening. He could not believe that Guinevere was guilty, but only that morning a wicked rumor had reached his ears that his wife and his beloved knight Sir Lancelot were in love with each other and plotting treason against him. It was also being said that the Queen was trying to poison anyone who might stand in their way – and certainly Gawain, as his nephew, was in direct line to the throne.

Whatever the truth of the matter, it was his duty as King to see that justice was done. He had no choice but to arrest the Queen on a charge of murder, but he was determined to give her a fair trial. He called together all the knights to gather around the Round Table, and at a solemn meeting it was agreed that Guinevere's guilt or

innocence should be determined by a trial by single combat. Both the Queen and Sir Patrice's kin would choose a champion to fight for them. If the Queen's champion overcame the knight chosen on behalf of Sir Patrice, then she would be judged innocent. If her champion lost and she was proved guilty, then Guinevere would be burnt at the stake, like any other poisoner.

Sir Mador, convinced of the Queen's guilt, immediately volunteered to fight on behalf of his dead cousin.

"Prepare yourself to do battle fifteen days from now," said Arthur. "Then, if any knight comes forward to be the Queen's champion, you will fight together in single combat, and God will decide the outcome. And if no knight comes forward to fight for the Queen, or if she is found guilty, she will be publicly burnt at the stake."

By now all the knights had been persuaded that the Queen was guilty, and no one would come forward to fight for her. Arthur began to despair. "Where is Sir Lancelot?" he demanded. "If he were here, he would surely fight for you." And he reproached the Queen for having quarrelled with her faithful knight and driven him from the court.

Poor Guinevere wept, and longed for her lover to come and rescue her. She had no idea where Lancelot was, and for many days it seemed as if she was doomed to die without any trial. But at last Sir Bors, Lancelot's cousin, came forward and offered to fight for her. The Queen was glad to accept him as her champion – although she knew that it was only for love of Sir Lancelot that he did this, and not because he thought her innocent.

All too soon the day came when the Queen's trial was to take place. Guinevere was brought out and tied to the stake, for she would be burnt on the pyre immediately if Sir Mador overthrew her champion. She held her head high and showed no fear, though she had good cause to dread the outcome of the battle. For although Sir Bors was a good and brave knight, he was not very skilful at deeds of arms, and she hardly dared to hope that he would overthrow her accuser.

When the King had taken his seat, Sir Mador rode out and swore his oath. "I swear that it was the Queen who poisoned my cousin, Sir Patrice, and I am here to avenge his death."

Then Sir Bors, as the Queen's champion, came and stood beside him. "And I," he said, "swear that Queen Guinevere is innocent of this crime, and I will prove that she is not guilty."

Just as Sir Bors and Sir Mador were about to meet in battle, a knight dressed in shining white armor galloped into the courtyard. His visor was down so that no one could recognize him, and neither could he be identified from his shield or spear, for he carried no device.

"Sir Knight, this is my fight," he said to Bors. "Withdraw, so that I may do battle for the Queen."

Then, raising his voice so that everyone could hear, he shouted, "I have come to fight for Queen Guinevere against her accusers. She is innocent of this wicked charge that has been brought against her, and I am here to prove it. Prepare yourself, Sir Mador, and we will soon see who is right."

The unknown knight rode at Sir Mador and attacked him so fiercely that the Queen's accuser was overthrown almost immediately, and obliged to yield to Guinevere's champion in order to save his life.

"Declare that Queen Guinevere is innocent or die," said the stranger, standing over his fallen opponent with his sword drawn.

"She is innocent," cried Sir Mador. "I retract my accusation against her."

The strange knight put his sword back into its sheath and threw back his visor. Then everyone saw that it was Sir Lancelot who had come to the Queen's rescue. Sir Bors, knowing that he was not the most skilful fighter, had sent a messenger to Lancelot to tell him of the trial that was to take place, and the gallant knight had arrived just in time to save his lady from the fate that awaited her.

A great shout went up from the people when they recognized Sir Lancelot. He went over to the stake and released Queen Guinevere, who wept now that her ordeal was over. She took Lancelot's hand and he led her over to her husband. Arthur came down the steps of his dais to meet her, and kissed her tenderly in front of all the people. He thanked Lancelot again and again for rescuing his wife.

"There is no need to thank me, my lord King," said Lancelot. "I am pleased to have been of service to my Queen. As you know, I swore to be her knight, and her knight only, for the whole of my life."

All the other knights now crowded round Sir Lancelot to welcome him back, and they begged Guinevere's pardon for having misjudged her. Then Lady Nimue, who had helped Arthur on several other occasions, appeared among them and said, "The Queen is indeed innocent of the death of Sir Patrice. It was Sir Pinel de Savage who poisoned the fruit, but he has now escaped out of the country."

The knights were even more ashamed of their suspicions when they heard Lady Nimue's words, and for a time their loyalty to the King and Queen was as strong as it had ever been. However Guinevere, although she remained aloof from court matters, did not trust Mordred and knew that it would not be long before his evil influence was at work again.

THE DECLINE
OF CAMELOT

WINTER TOOK its hold on Camelot, and as the hours of daylight shortened, the cold and darkness reflected the evil that had begun to stir the court once more. Christmas that year was a joyless occasion. Camelot was no longer the united and happy place it used to be, and a cloud of suspicion seemed to be cast over the festivities.

When spring arrived at last and the weather grew warm and sunny, Guinevere was determined to forget the gloom of the past months. She longed to ride out into the green woods and fields and see everything growing young and fresh again. On May Day she chose ten Knights of the Round Table and told them that she would ride out with them into the woods and fields near Camelot.

"You must come on horseback," she said, "dressed all in green. And I will bring with me ten ladies."

So the knights, attended by squires, rode out without their armor, wearing the green attire of woodmen. The ladies and their maids looked as delicate and colorful as butterflies, dressed in gowns of gossamer silk and with flowers entwined in their hair. Determined to put aside their daily worries this carefree group set off into the woods, their bridles jingling in tune with their merry laughter and songs. After they had gone some distance they came to a sunlit clearing, and here they stopped to dance around the maypole and crown Guinevere Queen of the May with a garland of wild flowers.

When the happy party became hungry the pages set out a picnic on white linen cloths: fresh white bread, sweetmeats and fruit; and large jugs of wine, which made everyone drowsy in the warm afternoon. There was a great deal of flirting between the knights and the ladies, and Guinevere watched them indulgently. Although the Queen's beloved knight, Sir Lancelot, had declined to join her for such frivolous enjoyment, he was now back at court, where he continued to do good deeds and to serve King Arthur loyally.

On the same day that Guinevere went a-maying in the woods, a knight called Sir Urre arrived at Camelot, carried in a litter. This brave and gallant knight had travelled all over the world fighting for good causes. One day, in a tournament in Spain, he fought against a knight whose name was Sir Alphegus, and overthrew and killed him. He slew him in a fair fight, but the knight's mother, who was a sorceress, was so angry at her son's death that she swore to take revenge. Sir Urre had received seven wounds from his opponent's spear, and the sorceress put a spell on him so that these wounds would never heal, unless they were touched by the best knight in the world.

For many months Sir Urre had been in great pain, for no doctor was able to cure

him. At last his mother and sister decided to set out on pilgrimage with him to all the courts of Europe to look for the best knight in the world. They travelled through many countries, and at each castle or palace they visited they begged the knights to touch the wounds to see if they might be healed. They journeyed for seven years, and Sir Urre's wounds were touched by many knights and kings and noblemen, but no help was found anywhere. It seemed as though they would never discover the best knight in the world.

Still Sir Urre's mother did not lose heart, but boarded a ship and sailed overseas, and eventually the little party arrived at Camelot. When Arthur heard the story of her fruitless search, his heart filled with pity for her and her son, and he ordered all his knights to touch Sir Urre's wounds, to see if by any chance there might be one among them who could make the sick man well again.

"If Sir Galahad were here he would certainly be healed," the King said. "But unfortunately he is dead, and I am not sure whether there is now any knight in my court who is worthy to be called the best knight in the world. Nevertheless, every man here will lay their hands on him, and I myself will touch him first to encourage the others to do the same."

Then Arthur touched the wounds of the sick man, and one after another every man present touched the body of Sir Urre.

"Where is Sir Lancelot?" asked the King when all the knights who had tried to heal Sir Urre had failed. "Has he ridden out with the Queen?"

At that moment Lancelot came riding into the courtyard of the castle. He dismounted from his horse and greeted the King, and then Arthur told him the story of Sir Urre, and how he and all the knights present had tried to heal him.

"You, too, must touch his wounds as we have done," said Arthur.

Lancelot hung back. "No, my lord King," he said, "I would no longer dare to call myself the best knight in the world. If so many other knights and noblemen have failed, I cannot hope to succeed."

"You have no choice in this matter," said Arthur. "I command you to touch Sir Urre. I have promised his mother that every knight of my court will try to heal him."

Sir Urre tried to raise himself from the litter. Stretching out his hands towards Lancelot, he pleaded with him to try, "I beg you, Sir Knight, in God's name, to touch my wounds and see if you can cure me."

Lancelot could not refuse this pitiful appeal. "I wish to God that I could help you," he said, "but I know that I am not worthy to do such a deed. However, I must do as my lord King commands."

So Lancelot knelt down beside Sir Urre, and when he had prayed, he laid his hands on each of the seven wounds. As he touched them, they were healed. Sir Urre rose from his litter, and for the first time in seven years stood up on his feet.

When the King and Sir Urre's mother saw this miracle they fell down on their knees and gave thanks to God. But Lancelot hid his face in his hands and wept. Then

149

Arthur became silent too, for he remembered how on his very first day Lancelot had healed a wounded knight in the same way. And Lady Nimue had prophesied that Lancelot would do another such deed, his last before the decline of Camelot.

Meanwhile, Guinevere and her companions prepared to return to the castle. Now, unknown to the Queen, a certain knight called Sir Meliagrance had loved her for many years and longed to have her for his own. He had watched for a chance to steal her from Arthur, but Guinevere was always surrounded by knights in armor, and usually Sir Lancelot rode at her side. When Meliagrance heard that morning that the Queen was riding out with only a few unarmed attendants, he thought that his chance had come at last. He called together his men-at-arms and archers and laid an ambush for Guinevere. As the happy revellers made their way back through the woods his troops leapt out and surrounded them.

"You traitor knight!" cried Queen Guinevere when she realized what had happened. "Remember that you are a king's son and a Knight of the Round Table. You bring dishonor on the whole order of knighthood."

"I care nothing for all of that," Sir Meliagrance declared. "I have loved you for many years and I have never before had such a chance as this."

The ten knights who rode with Queen Guinevere tried to defend her, but as they wore no armor and were hopelessly outnumbered, it was not long before all of them lay wounded on the ground.

"Sir Meliagrance, do not slay my knights," begged Guinevere. "I will go with you if you promise not to harm them further."

"Madam, for your sake I will spare them. I will have them carried into my castle and their wounds will be attended to."

150

So Guinevere and her knights and ladies were taken to the castle of Sir Meliagrance. On the way one of the squires managed to break away and galloped at full speed towards Camelot. Meliagrance saw him riding off, and ordered the archers to shoot at him. But the arrows fell wide of their mark, and the boy arrived safely at the court not long after Lancelot had healed Sir Urre.

When he heard the squire's story Lancelot leapt onto his horse at once. "I must rescue the Queen. I cannot rest until she is safe," he cried. And without waiting to summon any of the other knights he set off in pursuit of Sir Meliagrance.

Before he had gone very far a band of archers appeared in front of him, and when they saw Lancelot riding so furiously towards them, they drew their bows and let the arrows fly. The arrows glanced harmlessly off Lancelot's armor, but his horse was shot dead beneath him.

So Lancelot had to continue along the road on foot. He rushed at the archers with his spear, but they scattered immediately and he could not catch up with them because his armor was so heavy. Without his horse he had no hope of reaching the castle, but he dared not leave any of his arms behind, in case Sir Meliagrance had laid more traps.

Just then Lancelot saw a cart approaching, and he called out to the woodmen who were driving it, "Stop, friends, and let me ride in your cart."

"Where are you going?" one of them asked.

"To Sir Meliagrance's castle," Lancelot replied. "I will give you fifty pieces of gold if you will take me there."

Such riches were more than the two men could hope to earn in a lifetime, so they readily agreed to help. Hoisting the armored knight up onto the cart, they covered him with a pile of wood. Then they turned the cart around, and lashing up the horses set off at a fast pace towards the castle where Guinevere was now held captive.

Sir Meliagrance had prepared a chamber for the Queen at the top of a high tower. It was richly furnished with beautifully carved wood furniture, and heavy silk rugs covered the walls and floors. Guinevere was looking out of the window of her luxurious prison when she saw the cart pulling into the courtyard. She watched idly as the two men began to unload the wood, and then started in surprise when a fully-armored knight clambered heavily to the ground.

The Queen knew instantly that it was Sir Lancelot from the device on his shield. "Oh, I knew he would come," she murmured. "I knew he would come!"

"Where is the Queen?" cried Lancelot in a loud voice that rang throughout the whole castle. "Where is that traitor Meliagrance? Come out and fight!"

When Sir Meliagrance heard Lancelot's angry voice he was far too terrified to come out and do battle with him. He ran to the Queen and flung himself on his knees before her, begging her to forgive him and to intercede for him with Lancelot.

"Tell him I have done you no harm!" he begged. "Tell him I have taken care of your knights. Tell him that he can have my castle and everything in it, and I will be his slave for ever more, if he will only spare my life!"

Guinevere drew her robes contemptuously away from Meliagrance's imploring hands. "You are not worth fighting with!" she said disdainfully.

Then she called down to Lancelot from the open window. "Meliagrance has done me no harm, and enough blood has been spilt for one day. Put away your sword and make peace with him."

Lancelot was reluctant to allow the treacherous knight to remain unpunished, but he was so relieved to find the Queen safe and unhurt that he could not refuse her request. So instead of killing the terrified knight in cold blood, he agreed to do battle with him in full armor, at Camelot in the presence of King Arthur.

Sir Meliagrance was greatly relieved at this turn of events and began to treat Guinevere and Lancelot as if they were honored guests. As night was falling, they stayed in the castle, and early the next day Arthur arrived with a company of knights. When Guinevere told her husband what had happened, the King agreed that Meliagrance should fight a duel with Lancelot.

"It will take place one week from today," he ordered, "in the meadow between Camelot and the river. And if either of them fails to turn up, then he will be known as the most shameful knight in all of Britain."

Arthur took the Queen back with him to Camelot, and the wounded knights were carried there on litters.

"Sir Knight," said Meliagrance to Lancelot as they had left, "I trust there is no hate between us now? I have always admired your deeds of chivalry, and it would give me great pleasure if you would stay a while and let me prepare a feast in your honor."

When evening came Meliagrance led the way to the dining hall, and Lancelot did not see that there was a trapdoor in the darkened passage. As he trod on it, the trapdoor opened under his feet and he fell down into a black vault filled with straw.

Lancelot was now Meliagrance's prisoner, and he cursed himself for being so easily tricked. With each passing day that he languished in the vault he grew more and more anxious that he would not be able to escape in time for the duel.

Every evening a pretty maiden brought the wretched knight food and water; and every evening she said to him, "Good Sir Lancelot, if you will promise to love me and be my lord, I will set you free from this prison."

Lancelot knew he could not promise this: he loved only Queen Guinevere and would never fight for any other lady. "I cannot buy my freedom at such a price," he said to her gently. "King Arthur will know that only treachery would keep me from Camelot when the day of the battle comes."

But on the morning of the day when he was due to fight with Sir Meliagrance, the girl came to Sir Lancelot again and said, "Noble Lancelot, I have loved you in vain. Give me just one kiss, and I will set you free."

This seemed such a small price to pay that Lancelot did as the maiden asked, but he kissed her with such lack of feeling that she burst into tears. "My kiss means nothing to you," she sobbed, "it is true that you love only Guinevere." However, she kept her part of the bargain, and led Lancelot out of the castle and fetched him his armor and a horse to ride.

Meanwhile Arthur and Guinevere, with many knights and ladies, were gathered in the great meadow at Camelot to see the duel. The hour came, and there was no sign

of Sir Lancelot. Sir Meliagrance swaggered about, boasting that he was the best knight in Britain and Lancelot was merely a coward. He was about to claim victory by default when suddenly a cry went up and Sir Lancelot was seen galloping towards them. He pulled up in front of the King and told how the treacherous Meliagrance had tricked him. Everyone began to mock Sir Meliagrance until at last he seized his spear and cried, "Defend yourself!" to Sir Lancelot.

Then the two knights drew away to the ends of the meadow and at a given signal rode at each other furiously. Sir Lancelot struck Meliagrance so hard that he fell backwards over his horse's tail. Then Lancelot dismounted, drew his sword, waited until Meliagrance was on his feet again, and attacked him fiercely. Meliagrance tried to escape, but Lancelot struck him so hard that his helmet was split in half. With one last stroke Lancelot sliced off his head, and that was the end of Meliagrance.

King Arthur thanked Lancelot in front of the whole court for rescuing the Queen, and for a time there was peace and harmony again at Camelot. Lancelot could not forgive himself for allowing such danger to threaten his beloved Guinevere, and now he was never far from her side. Mordred continually watched them both to see if he could catch them in each other's arms, but they took great care to be discreet.

Then one day Sir Agravain, who was Gawain's brother and a close follower of Mordred, happened to overhear Guinevere arranging to meet Lancelot at sundown.

He went at once to tell Sir Mordred, and the two men hid themselves that evening behind a privet hedge in her private garden. Before long the Queen appeared and walked up and down among the rose-beds, stopping now and then to smell the flowers. She walked alone for a while, and then Sir Lancelot came to join her.

Guinevere's face flushed with pleasure as he tenderly kissed her hand. "Sir Lancelot, I have never thanked you properly for rescuing me from Meliagrance."

"There is no need for thanks, my lady," murmured Lancelot. "There is nothing in the world that I would not do for you."

"Oh Lancelot, Lancelot," said Guinevere softly, "I have loved you since the very first day you came to Camelot, when I was little more than a girl, and Arthur's bride."

"I fell in love with you on that day, too," said Lancelot. "And for all these years I have fought against that love – but in vain."

"Lancelot," said Guinevere, hesitating for a moment before she continued. "Lancelot, more than anything else in the world I would like to be your lady. Come to my chamber tomorrow at midnight...."

"Guinevere, my lady, my love ... are you sure that this is what you want?"

Guinevere nodded. She took Lancelot's face gently between her hands and gazed lovingly into his eyes before kissing him passionately on the lips. Then she turned and went away through the twilight. Lancelot stood motionless for several minutes after she had gone, and then he too left the garden.

Mordred turned to Sir Agravain with a wicked gleam in his eyes. "Our time has come at last," he said triumphantly.

Later that night, in an upper room of the castle, Mordred, Agravain and Gawain sat around a flickering candle that threw black shadows onto the bare stone walls.

"Brother Agravain," protested Sir Gawain, "I do not want to hear any more of this. I will have nothing to do with your wicked plan."

"Come on, Gawain," said Agravain persuasively. "We all know that Lancelot loves the Queen and that he would like to overthrow Arthur and make himself king. And he will not stop at that – you are the King's eldest nephew, and a possible heir. What do you think he will do to you? We only have to tell the King that Lancelot will be visiting his wife's chamber at midnight...."

"If you don't want to join us in this," said Mordred quietly, "then Agravain and I will go and tell the King ourselves."

And so Agravain and Mordred went to the King and told him what they had overheard in the Queen's private garden. At first Arthur refused to believe them. "You will pay with your heads if you have come to me with lies and slander!" he said angrily.

But as he listened to them some more Arthur thought about how distracted Guinevere had been lately; how her mind always seemed to be on other things – and how she no longer welcomed him to her bedchamber. And it was certainly true that rumors had been circulating for some time; even Arthur was aware of this.

At last the King agreed that Sir Mordred and Sir Agravain should keep watch that night outside the Queen's bedchamber. When they had gone, Sir Gawain found him sitting alone in the great empty hall with tears running down into his grey beard.

Sir Lancelot meanwhile was entertaining his cousin, Sir Bors. As midnight approached he rose to his feet and said, "I bid you goodnight, cousin, I must go to the Queen."

"Lancelot, I advise you not to go," said Bors.

"Why not?" asked Lancelot.

"I think that Sir Mordred is plotting to betray you, and indeed to bring ruin to us all at Camelot."

"I have given Guinevere my word," Lancelot replied. "Do not worry – the night is dark and everyone has gone to their beds."

Lancelot wrapped his cloak around him, and putting his sword under his arm, went off through the dark corridors to Queen Guinevere's chamber. Bors, watching him leave, was full of foreboding. He roused his brother, Sir Lionel, and together they went down to the courtyard.

Lancelot and Guinevere had been together for only a few minutes when there was a loud knocking at the door.

"You traitor, Sir Lancelot! Now you are caught!" shouted Mordred in a voice loud enough to wake everyone in the castle.

Guinevere looked at Lancelot with fear in her eyes. "My lord," she whispered, "We are both betrayed."

"Traitor! Come out of the Queen's bedchamber!" shouted Agravain, beating vigorously on the door. By now several other knights had appeared in their nightshirts, anxious to see what was causing such a commotion. Mordred struck at the door with the hilt of his sword and rattled the bolt that held it fast.

"Open the door or we will break it down!" he shouted.

Inside the chamber Lancelot took the trembling Queen in his arms. "My lady," he said, "I have no choice but to open the door. Whatever comes of this, remember that I will always be true." He wound his cloak round his arm, unbarred the door and opened it a little way.

Sir Agravain rushed forward to attack Lancelot, but he warded off the blow and struck Agravain so forcefully on his head that he fell to the floor dead. Quickly Lancelot dragged him into the room and barred the door once more. Then he stripped the armor off the dead knight and put it on himself.

"Traitor knight! Come out I say! There is no hope for you now!" bellowed Sir Mordred.

Then Lancelot flung the door open and rushed out at the assembled knights. Slashing wildly with his sword he made his way down the staircase and out into the courtyard, where Sir Bors and Sir Lionel were waiting with horses. The three cousins fled into the forest and rode to the Joyous Isle, where they were soon joined by other knights who supported Sir Lancelot.

THE QUEEN'S TRIAL

JUST AS Merlin the magician had prophesied, fate was now taking its inevitable course. The noble fellowship of the Round Table was irretrievably divided, for Lancelot was soon joined by other knights who preferred to ally themselves to his cause rather than go along with Mordred's evil scheming. Sir Lancelot, with his cousins Sir Lionel and Sir Bors, and a band of loyal followers, took refuge at the Joyous Isle, where a long time ago Lancelot had lived for a while with Elaine and his infant son Galahad. It almost broke Lancelot's heart to desert his King, for he loved Arthur, who had given him his knighthood and who up to now had shown him nothing but courtesy and kindness.

As Lancelot and his companions rode away from Camelot, Mordred came down in anger from the Queen's bedchamber and found the King still sitting with Sir Gawain in the Great Hall.

"Well?" said Arthur. "Where is Sir Lancelot? Did you not find him in the Queen's chamber?"

"He was there all right, just as we said he would be, and he was unarmed. But he killed Sir Agravain and then took his armor and fought his way out."

"Ah," said Arthur sadly, "he is indeed a brave and gallant knight. I regret that he is now against me, for many knights will side with him, and this will be the end of our noble fellowship of the Round Table."

"What about the Queen?" said Mordred. "She should be sent for trial, and if she is found guilty of treason, she must die at the stake."

Arthur started to weep again: he knew that he would be powerless to change the sentence. Throughout his reign he had always insisted on justice for all his people, whatever their rank, and this included the Queen.

"We do not know that she is guilty," said Gawain gently. "Perhaps she sent for Lancelot to thank him again for saving her from Meliagrance."

The trial took place in the Great Hall at Camelot, where there had been so many happy gatherings in the past. The court listened gravely as the Queen, looking frail and tired, was accused of high treason. She was found guilty and sentenced to be burnt at the stake. Lancelot, too, was condemned in his absence: if he were captured he would be ceremonially stripped of his knighthood and hanged.

With a heavy heart Arthur said to his nephew Gawain, "In the morning you will lead Queen Guinevere to her execution."

"Not I, my lord King," cried Sir Gawain, "I will not be the one who leads her to the pyre."

"Yet she had a hand in the death of your brother, Agravain."

"I was always warning Agravain not to get involved in underhand plots. In any case, Lancelot was unarmed, so I forgive him for Agravain's death."

"Then your brothers, Gareth and Gaheris, must do it instead," insisted Arthur.

These two knights did not want to escort the Queen either. They knew that Lancelot would try and rescue Guinevere, and in preventing him they might well cause him harm. Both of them admired the gallant knight, and Sir Gareth especially loved him, for he had been dubbed a knight by Sir Lancelot.

"Sir," they said reluctantly, "we will do as you command us, but we will go unarmed and dressed in mourning clothes."

So Gareth and Gaheris led Guinevere to the stake, and Arthur remained in an upper room that overlooked the courtyard. He was sure that Lancelot would try to rescue the Queen, and sure enough, just as the pyre was about to be lit the gallant knight came thundering into the courtyard with his supporters. Slashing at anyone who got in his way, Lancelot rode straight up to the stake and cut Guinevere free. Then he lifted her onto his horse and galloped out of the castle as quickly as he had come.

Arthur breathed a great sigh of relief. The two people he loved best in the world were now free from immediate danger. But unfortunately the unarmed Gareth and Gaheris, who were nearest to the Queen, had been struck down and killed by Lancelot in the confusion.

Sir Gawain, who had not cared too much about Agravain, was grief-stricken when he saw that his other two brothers were dead. Turning to Arthur he demanded that a army should be sent to destroy Lancelot and his supporters.

"I swear to God that I will not rest until Lancelot and I meet face to face and one of us is slain," he cried. "I will never forgive him for killing Gareth and Gaheris."

Lancelot carried Queen Guinevere deep into the forest until they came to a nunnery. "My lady," he said tenderly, "it is best that I leave you here in this place of safety. I fear that I shall never again be at peace with King Arthur, but if I am spared from the conflict that is sure to follow, I will come for you again."

Guinevere wept bitterly but saw that it was the honorable thing to do.

Lancelot fled with his loyal band of followers to Benoic in northern France, where he was born. Sir Gawain urged Arthur to follow him, and so many knights sided with Gawain that Arthur was forced to declare war on Sir Lancelot. He gathered together an army and left for France, leaving Mordred to rule in Britain while he was away.

When the King's army arrived at Benoic they camped beside a river and settled down to lay siege to the castle. But Lancelot, who had seen them coming, had sent Sir Lionel and Sir Bors with a number of men into a nearby forest, in order to surprise Arthur's forces. He instructed them that when they saw a red flag raised above the fortress, they were to make a frontal attack on the King's men; those who had remained in the castle would make a sortie at the same moment, so that Arthur's army would be assailed on both sides.

When the flag was seen by those lying in wait in the forest, they rode out onto the plain as quietly as possible, while Lancelot gave the command for the castle gates to be opened. But one of Arthur's men heard the sound of the horses' hooves and came out of the camp to investigate. He came face to face with Sir Bors, who spurred on his horse and struck his opponent so hard that he fell to the ground. The other men coming after him began tearing down the King's pavilions and flattening whatever they came across. Hearing this commotion Arthur and his barons quickly armed themselves. It was not long before fierce fighting had broken out on all sides, and continued unabated for the rest of the day.

The war continued for several months, and many brave men were killed on both sides. It looked as though the conflict would never end. Every day Sir Gawain stood at the castle gates and called to Lancelot to come out and fight with him in single combat. At first Lancelot took no notice of this challenge: he knew that he was stronger than Gawain and could not bear the thought of fighting to the death against someone who had once been his friend. But eventually he could bear Gawain's taunts no longer, and came out to do battle.

It was a long fight, for Gawain was determined to kill Lancelot if he could, while Lancelot did not want to do more than overthrow Gawain. For a long time the onlookers could not tell which way the battle would go, but in the end Lancelot struck Gawain such a blow that he fell to the ground. Then, as Gawain lay there expecting the other knight to finish the fight and kill him, Lancelot put his sword back in its sheath and walked away.

"Why are you withdrawing?" Gawain called after him. "Come back, traitor knight, and kill me. I swear that if you leave me like this, I will not rest until I have fought with you again."

"So be it," said Lancelot, "but, whatever happens, I will never slay a fallen knight."

So the war went on, while Gawain recovered from his wounds and fretted and

fumed to do battle with Lancelot again. It was more than a month before he was well enough to bear arms, and even then he was not able to issue another challenge, for such grave news came from England that Arthur was forced to lift his siege of Lancelot's castle and hurry back to defend his kingdom.

Sir Mordred, who had been left in charge of Britain, had turned traitor. As soon as Arthur had gone, he summoned the remaining barons and knights to him, and held

court and made many gifts, until he had won over most of the nobles. His spies had found Guinevere at the nunnery where Sir Lancelot had left her, and he brought her back to court. Now he planned to get himself crowned, with her as his Queen.

In order to achieve this end he forged a letter with King Arthur's seal. This was sent to one of the bishops, who read it out to the assembled barons and knights in the presence of the Queen.

I greet you as one who has been mortally wounded at Lancelot's hand. All my men have already been killed and slaughtered. For the sake of peace I order you to crown Sir Mordred as King of all Britain, and I beg him to take Queen Guinevere, my widow, as his wife.
Arthur, King of all Britain

When the letter was read out Mordred pretended to be very distressed, but the Queen was not quite convinced that its contents were true. Despite the grave risk to her own safety, for she was still under the threat of execution for treason, she sent a messenger secretly to France to find out whether Arthur was indeed dead. The King, on learning of Mordred's treachery, immediately called together the remains of his army and set sail for Dover.

The people of Dover received their King joyfully because they had thought he was dead. When Mordred heard that Arthur had learned of his treachery and was hurrying home to regain his crown, he raised an army and marched to Dover. The forces of father and son engaged in a bloody battle. Many good and loyal knights were slain, as brother fought brother and cousin fought cousin. Mordred's army was badly beaten and he retreated to gather more men and prepare for another battle.

At the end of that day's fighting Arthur rode around the battlefield to see which knights had been killed. He found Gawain lying in a pool of blood, half-dead from severe wounds. The King had his beloved nephew carried to his tent, and laid in

his own bed. Gawain's injuries were tenderly dressed, but it was too late to save his life.

"All this trouble is my fault," said Gawain sadly. "It has only happened because of my feud with Lancelot. If Lancelot were here, your enemies would never have dared to raise an army against you."

Knowing that his end was near, Gawain called for writing materials, and with the little strength that he had left, he wrote a letter to Lancelot begging him to come with his followers to rescue the King.

Sir Lancelot, best and bravest knight:

For the love we once all shared, I beg you and your noble companions to put aside past differences and come back to Britain to fight for our King. He is in danger of losing his life at the hands of Mordred, his traitorous son, who plots to usurp his throne and take Queen Guinevere as his wife.

I am close to death from wounds received in battle. By the time you read this my life will be at its end. Please pray for my soul.

Gawain of Orkney

When Sir Lancelot received Gawain's letter a few days later, he immediately prepared to return to Britain, hoping that he would be in time to help Arthur rout the evil Mordred and his army.

THE LAST BATTLE

Aᴛᴇʀ ᴛʜᴇ battle at Dover, Mordred fled away defeated, but soon news came that he had raised another army and was marching into the west country, raiding the lands of all those who would not ally themselves to his cause. So the King marched his troops towards Cornwall and arrived at Camlann, near the mysterious place where, so many years before, Merlin had brought him to receive his sword Excalibur from the Lady of the Lake.

Scarcely a mile away Mordred waited for the King with a huge army of knights and men-at-arms. He had more men than Arthur, formed in twenty battalions. All his best knights were in the last one, which he led himself. He planned to fight against Arthur with this battalion, because his spies had told him that the King would be leading the last battalion of his army.

That night Arthur could not sleep. He knew that in the morning there would be another great battle and many more brave knights would be killed. And he also feared that this was, as Merlin had prophesied, the last battle of all. Already the Saxon warriors had heard about the civil war in Britain and were starting to invade once again. The hard-won peace of Arthur's reign would soon be no more.

Arthur tossed and turned on his bed in the royal tent, sometimes asleep and sometimes awake, and it seemed to him that the dead Sir Gawain rode up to him in a vision. He was attended by a train of fair ladies for whom he had fought. Throughout his life Gawain had always been known as the champion of ladies.

"Do not fight tomorrow, Uncle," said the armored ghost. "Call a truce for a month. If you delay awhile Sir Lancelot and his knights will come to your aid and together you will defeat the usurper."

Then Sir Gawain and the ladies vanished again, and Arthur rose from his bed and called together his counsellors to tell them of his dream. They advised him to arrange the truce as the ghost of Sir Gawain had suggested.

So it was arranged that King Arthur and Sir Mordred, each accompanied by fourteen knights, would meet at a spot between the two armies. Because Arthur did not trust Mordred, he gave an order to his men, "If you see a drawn sword, charge fiercely and slay that traitor Sir Mordred, for I do not trust him."

While he was speaking, Mordred was also addressing his knights, "If you see a drawn sword, attack and slay all of Arthur's men! I do not trust this truce, for I know that the King is eager to get his revenge on me."

Both parties advanced into the middle ground, and the agreement was drawn up and signed by both of them. Then wine was brought and passed round as a token of good faith. As the knights were drinking, an adder slid out of the grass and bit one of

166

Mordred's knights on the heel. Without thinking he drew his sword to kill it, and as he did so the blade caught the sunlight so that both watching armies saw its gleam.

A great shout went up from both sides, and the next moment they were charging at each other across the plain of Camlann. The men in the front battalions came together with such violence that they skewered each other's bodies with their lances, the blades passing right through them. Then when their lances were broken they fought with swords, delivering such great blows that helmets were crushed and shields split into pieces. Horses reared and threw their riders, and many knights continued fighting on foot, pitting their strength against their opponents with a clash of steel on steel.

Battalion after battalion fell wounded and dying. All through the battle King Arthur fought bravely, riding straight into the ranks of Mordred's forces, searching for his traitorous son. The fighting raged all day long and there was terrible slaughter on both sides. When darkness began to fall Arthur struggled to see which of his good and loyal knights remained alive, and discovered to his horror that only two survived – Sir Bedivere and his brother, Sir Lucan.

"Are all my brave knights gone?" he murmured in disbelief, as he looked sadly around the bloody battlefield. Then he saw Sir Mordred leaning on his spear among a pile of dead bodies.

"This is my chance to rid the world of my traitorous son," cried Arthur to Sir Lucan.

"Do not linger, my lord, I beg you," said Lucan. "Remember Sir Gawain's warning. Leave him and escape while you are still alive."

"Never!" shouted Arthur, and sprang at Mordred crying, "Traitor! Turn and fight if you dare, for now I will kill you!"

He raised Excalibur in both hands and struck Mordred on the head with such force that the blade cut through his helmet and sent him staggering to the ground. Mordred knew that he was fatally wounded, but summoning up all his strength, grasped his spear and plunged it deep into Arthur's body.

Then Mordred groaned and fell back dead. "You should have died as soon as you were born," said Arthur bitterly.

Seeing that the King had fallen, Sir Lucan and Sir Bedivere hurried to his side.

"Carry me away from this stinking battlefield so that I may breathe some clear air," said Arthur.

The two brothers lifted the dying King up in their arms. Not far away there was a lake, and in the gathering gloom they could just see the ruins of a small chapel that stood close beside it. There would be shelter for the King there, they thought, and together they carried Arthur and laid him gently down on the floor.

But Sir Lucan had been seriously wounded in the battle, and the effort of lifting the King was too much for him. The blood gushed out of his wound and he fell to the ground and died. Bedivere wept when he saw that his brother was dead, but his tears could not bring Sir Lucan back to life, so he turned again to the King, to see if he was still conscious.

The King was also badly wounded, and knew that his end had come. He raised himself feebly on his elbow and gazed around him, and when he saw the lake he suddenly remembered where he was. It was the very spot where the Lady of the Lake had given him his sword so long ago, and as he recognized it he recalled the words that she had spoken to him: "Before you die, you must return the sword to me."

"Bedivere," said Arthur hoarsely, hardly able to speak. "Take my sword Excalibur from its sheath and and throw it into the lake. Then come back here and tell me what you have seen."

Sir Bedivere took the sword and carried it down to the water's edge. But when he looked at the wonderful hilt, encrusted with jewels, temptation overcame him.

"Why should I throw this beautiful sword into the lake?" he said to himself. "My lord King is weak and dying, he does not know what he is saying. If he were in his right mind, he would never ask me to throw away his magic sword. No good will come of it."

So instead of throwing the sword into the water, he hid it among the rushes at the side of the lake. Then he went back to the ruined chapel, and as he reached it, the King asked him eagerly, "Did you throw the sword into the water?"

Sir Bedivere said, untruthfully, "Yes, my lord King."

"And what did you see?"

"I saw nothing but the waves on the lake," said Bedivere.

"Then you are lying to me," said Arthur angrily. "If you had done as I asked, some sign would have followed. Do as I command you and throw Excalibur into the lake."

Bedivere was ashamed of himself for having kept back the sword, so he returned to the lake and retrieved the sword from the place where he had hidden it. But once more the rich sparkle of the jewels caught his eye, and he could not bring himself to throw the sword into the lake.

He hid Excalibur in the rushes again and told the King that he had done as he had been ordered.

"And what did you hear?" asked Arthur faintly.

"Sir, I heard nothing but the water lapping on the shore," replied Bedivere.

"Oh traitor knight! Twice you have lied to me. I never thought you would betray me for the hilt of a sword. Do as I command you, before I die."

Seeing that the King was now barely alive, Sir Bedivere was filled with remorse for deceiving him. He ran to the edge of the lake and flung Excalibur far out over the water. As the sword fell, an arm clad in white samite rose out of the lake and caught it by the hilt, waved it three times in the air, and then slowly vanished below the water. The Lady of the Lake had taken possession of her gift again.

When Sir Bedivere told Arthur what had happened, he was satisfied. "Now help me to the water's edge," he said. "My end is near and it is time that I was gone."

Sir Bedivere lifted the King in his arms and carried him down to the water's edge. As they reached the shore, a barge came gliding towards them. In it were three queens, all dressed in black mourning robes. One of the queens was the King's half-sister, Morgan le Fay, who no longer practised the black arts and had come to make her peace with Arthur. The second queen was another of Arthur's half-sisters, Margawse, the wife of King Lot of Orkney, and mother of his favorite nephew Sir Gawain. The third draped figure was the Lady of the Lake, guardian of the Vale of Avalon, which was to be Arthur's final resting place.

The three queens held out their arms, took the dying King from Sir Bedivere and laid him in their laps.

"You have waited too long, dear brother," said Morgan le Fay.

Then the barge moved slowly and silently away from the shore, steered by Lady Nimue who sat silent and motionless in the stern. And Sir Bedivere was left alone and desolate on the shore.

"What will become of me now, King Arthur?" he called after the departing barge. "Do not leave me here among my enemies."

"Look after yourself as best you can," came the faint reply, "for I am no longer able to help you. I must go to Avalon to be healed of my wound. If Britain has need of me, I will come again. And if you never hear of me again, pray for my soul."

With these last words King Arthur journeyed into the magic place where no mortal man may venture, and a mist descended on the lake at Avalon.

Some say that Arthur stayed too long and died of his wound in Avalon and that he was buried at Glastonbury with Guinevere beside him. But others say that he is still asleep in Avalon and will return in the hour of Britain's greatest need.

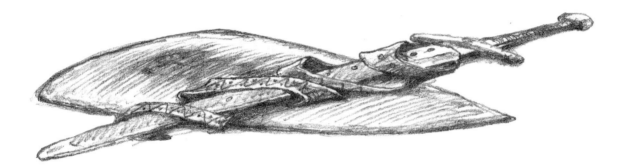